A CHANGE OF PROGRAM . . .

"GOOD MORNING," Smith keyed in crisply, as he did every morning, and waited for the computers to return the greeting.

The megaliths hummed and buzzed and bleeped, and then the screen changed color from dark green to steel gray, preparing to transmit.

"DOCTOR SMITH. CALL 555-8000."

He gasped.

"GOOD MORNING," he typed again.

"DOCTOR SMITH. CALL 555-8000."

He altered the mode. "CODE 041265124. TRANSMIT."

"DOCTOR SMITH. CALL 555-8000."

He was shaking. The sensation coursing through his body was the closest thing to rage he had ever felt. He took the machines back to their earliest, simplest memories.

"CODE 0641. GIVE 100 REAL NUMBERS IN BASE 10."

They clicked and whined. With the tack-tack of paper processing, a sheet of printout paper spilled onto Smith's desk.

"DOCTOR SMITH. CALL 555-8000. DOCTOR SMITH. CALL 555-8000. DOCTOR . . ."

Smith turned off the console. His palms were clammy. Someone had done the impossible. They had invaded the absolute privacy of the Folcroft computers.

THE DESTROYER SERIES:

#1 CREATED, THE DESTROYER
#2 DEATH CHECK
#3 CHINESE PUZZLE
#4 MAFIA FIX
#5 DR. QUAKE
#6 DEATH THERAPY
#7 UNION BUST
#8 SUMMIT CHASE
#9 MURDERER'S SHIELD
#10 TERROR SQUAD
#11 KILL OR CURE
#12 SLAVE SAFARI
#13 ACID ROCK
#14 JUDGMENT DAY
#15 MURDER WARD
#16 OIL SLICK
#17 LAST WAR DANCE
#18 FUNNY MONEY
#19 HOLY TERROR
#20 ASSASSIN'S PLAY-OFF
#21 DEADLY SEEDS
#22 BRAIN DRAIN
#23 CHILD'S PLAY
#24 KING'S CURSE
#25 SWEET DREAMS
#26 IN ENEMY HANDS

#27 THE LAST TEMPLE
#28 SHIP OF DEATH
#29 THE FINAL DEATH
#30 MUGGER BLOOD
#31 THE HEAD MEN
#32 KILLER CHROMOSOMES
#33 VOODOO DIE
#34 CHAINED REACTION
#35 LAST CALL
#36 POWER PLAY
#37 BOTTOM LINE
#38 BAY CITY BLAST
#39 MISSING LINK
#40 DANGEROUS GAMES
#41 FIRING LINE
#42 TIMBER LINE
#43 MIDNIGHT MAN
#44 BALANCE OF POWER
#45 SPOILS OF WAR
#46 NEXT OF KIN
#47 DYING SPACE
#48 PROFIT MOTIVE
#49 SKIN DEEP
#50 KILLING TIME
#51 SHOCK VALUE

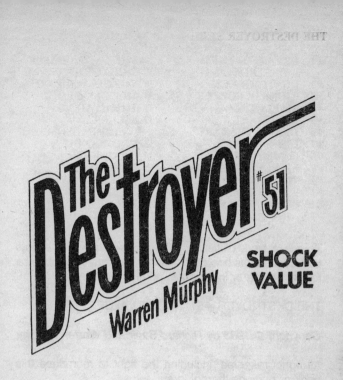

The Destroyer #51

SHOCK VALUE

Warren Murphy

PINNACLE BOOKS **NEW YORK**

THE DESTROYER #51: SHOCK VALUE

Copyright © 1983 by Richard Sapir and Warren Murphy

An original Pinnacle Books edition, published for the first time anywhere.

First printing, February 1983

ISBN: 0-523-41561-3

Cover illustration by Hector Garrido

Printed in the United States of America

PINNACLE BOOKS, INC.
1430 Broadway
New York, New York 10018

**For Pat Sellus and
for the House of Sinanju,
P.O. Box 1454, Secaucus, N.J. 07094**

SHOCK VALUE

Chapter One

Orville Peabody was watching television. Had his mind been operating correctly, he might have said that he liked television as well as anybody. Back home in the nondescript clapboard ranchstyle house in West Mahomset, Ohio, which he shared with his regulation homemaker wife and their requisite quota of average children, he had watched quite a bit of television. As a child, in another nondescript clapboard ranch-style house in West Mahomset, he had squeezed in regular doses of "Howdy Doody" and "Ted Mack's Amateur Hour" between his activities at Junior Achievers, Four-H, and the Boy Scouts. His taste had improved since then. Sometimes, back in West Mahomset, he even watched "Masterpiece Theatre."

He was not watching "Masterpiece Theatre" now. If Orville Peabody's mind had been operating correctly, he might have questioned what he *was* watching, which was a daytime soap opera titled "Ways of Our Days," featuring an inane cast of adolescent rock musicians turned actors. He might have questioned the place where he was watching it, which was about as far from West Mahomset as you could get.

He might also have questioned the identities of the two men who flanked him on either side, each gazing intently into his own silent television set, listening through earphones to the greedy squeals of a game show audience and violins in a rerun of an Old Lassie movie.

But Orville Peabody's mind was not operating correctly. It was drinking in each millisecond of "Ways of Our Days" with a thirst unequalled in the annals of telecommunications. It was absorbing information with an intensity that left Peabody breathless and expectant. It was extracting from the beating light in front of him a message so clear that it stood out like a shining nugget, hard and inviolate, against the vague flapping images on the television screen.

It was telling him his destiny.

And so Orville Peabody, in his glorious moment of revelation, did not wonder why he was sitting in a darkened room on a tropical island, his skin brown from unremembered days in the sun, huddled beside two strangers who might have been sitting, unmoving, beside him for hours or days or weeks for all he knew. Nothing mattered now. He had a mission. It had come to him through the television, and it was not to be questioned. Orville Peabody was at peace.

Smiling like a prophet who has viewed the future of man and found it good, he rose from his contoured chair and turned off the set. The two other men in the room never glanced his way. Without a thought for the stiff muscles brought on by the hours of sitting, he walked over to the small closet in the room and put on his suit jacket. Everything was in place: his wallet, containing the forty-two dollars he had left West Mahomset with; three credit cards; a passport; photographs of his wife and kids; and a Swiss Army knife. His father had given him the knife for his tenth birthday, and Orville carried it wherever he went. "Just in case one of those muggers comes to West Mahomset with any fancy ideas," he would tell his kids with a wink.

Outside, the sun was shining, fairly pelting cheer onto the narrow dirt roads of the primitive island where the land gave way to the rocks and the rocks to the wild sea. It would be a wonderful day for traveling. He walked the two miles to the small island airport and bought a ticket for Newfoundland, Canada.

"How will you be paying for this, sir?" asked the clerk behind the makeshift counter.

"Credit card," Peabody answered, smiling. Automatically he reached into his trouser pocket and placed the card on the counter.

"Very good, Mr. Gray," the clerk said. "Now, if you can show some other identification . . ."

He looked at the name on the card, Joshua Gray. But he was Orville Peabody. All of his cards said so. Warily he reached inside his pants pocket again.

Wait a second, he thought. He didn't keep anything inside his trousers pockets. His I.D. was

3

in his jacket. And yet his hand had gone immediately for the card bearing the name of Joshua Gray. His fingers reached around a small booklet.

"That's it," the clerk said, opening up the passport to Peabody's picture. Below it was the name Joshua Gray. Peabody stared at it, uncomprehending. The clerk was motioning somewhere off to the right. "Your plane's boarding now, Mr. Gray." she said. "Have a pleasant trip."

"Thank you," Peabody said, fingering the strange passport and credit card. How had they gotten there? And why was he going to Canada? For a moment he panicked, sweat suddenly popping up on his brow and streaming cold from his armpits.

"Are you all right?" The clerk's face showed alarm.

"Yes, yes." Peabody drew a deep breath and irritably snatched up the identification. The moment of fear passed. Whatever had prompted him to use a false card he hadn't known to be in his possession was, he decided, nothing of his choosing. There were greater forces at work in him now, and it was not his place to question them. He was going to St. John's, Newfoundland, because that was where he knew he must go to live out the pulsing, unreachable message in his brain. He was to go there under a false name, because that was what the message had decreed. He knew also that, once in St. John's, he would discard the Joshua Gray passport and credit card and book passage on still another flight under his own name.

He wondered, as he walked into the airport at St. John's, where that flight would take him.

He looked for a men's room. His hands mechanically stashed the false card and passport into a trash bin, then his feet walked in sure, brisk strides toward the BOAC counter.

"Rome, first class," he heard himself say, reaching automatically for his Orville Peabody identification inside his jacket pocket.

Rome?

"Ladies and gentlemen. We are now making our final descent into Leonardo Da Vinci airport. . . ."

He was lost. He had no business in Rome. Or in St. John's, Newfoundland. Or on that cheerfully anonymous tropical island where he had spent the last eternity since he had seen West Mahomset, Ohio.

Orville Peabody worked in a clothing store. He had graduated without distinction from the local high school. He had married the daughter of one of his parents' friends. His kids played in Little League and belonged to Cub Scouts. Sometimes he watched "Masterpiece Theater."

What the hell am I doing here? he thought.

But those were not the words his lips formed. What came out of his mouth was a request for directions to some place he'd never heard of. The man he had spoken to, a distinguished-looking white-haired gentleman, pointed to his right.

"Spanish Steps?" the white-haired man asked in a refined British accent. "Can't miss it. Beautiful sight. Early eighteenth century, you know. Magnificent architecture. Of course, you won't see much of that today. Some kind of rally going on. Leftists, no doubt. They're everywhere. A pack of troublemakers, if you ask my opinion."

"Pack of troublemakers," Peabody repeated, dazed.

"Well, I daresay you'll enjoy it all the same," the Englishman said with gruff cheer. "Spot of color for your holiday, what? Cheerio."

"Pack of troublemakers," Peabody chanted under his breath.

The rally was in full force. Angry young men and women squeezed together, cheering zealously as one of their number shouted something incomprehensible to Peabody on the ancient steps above the crowd. For a few moments he watched the speaker without emotion. It was, after all, a foreign language everybody was screeching in, and the press of unwashed bodies and writhing, violent movement made Peabody feel even more uncomfortable, if that was possible, than before.

It was bad enough to be in a strange country with no luggage, no friends, and no apparent reason to be there. But to be stuck in the middle of some hostile campus demonstration, surrounded by the kind of freewheeling loonies he'd cross the street to avoid back home in West Mahomset . . .

He squeezed his eyes shut. The revelation had been blinding. *Not the speaker, you dummy!* He nearly laughed aloud. Of course. He should have known it would come to him. The false I.D., the trip to Newfoundland, the flight to Rome, the Spanish Steps—it was all perfectly clear now, as clear as the message that had dawned, bright and unspoken, as he watched "Ways of Our Days" in that darkened room.

He was in Rome not to watch the speaker, but the *crowd*.

For in that crowd, he knew, would be a face. And that face would have a name, *Franco Abbrodani*. How Orville Peabody knew this face and its attendant name, he could not recall, since neither was familiar to him. But his brain, still operating independently, thrummed with the pleasure of anticipation. His heartbeat quickened. A thin bar of moisture glistened on his upper lip.

Perhaps the man named Abbrodani would be a friend. Perhaps he was part of the unknown mission Peabody had been sent on, Peabody's destiny. With an Italian villa, perhaps, and a table filled with spaghetti and dago red wine and maybe even a telephone so he could call the wife back in West Mahomset . . .

The thrumming wailed into a shriek. Peabody could hardly breathe. He was here . . . near . . . *now*.

With a grasp, he spotted the face he had been looking for. A face utterly unfamiliar to him, yet somehow as recognizable to him as any of the folks back home.

"Franco!" he shouted. A swarthy man in his late thirties wearing a combat jacket jerked his

7

eyes from the speaker on the steps and regarded the grinning, sweating American with suspicion. Peabody stretched out his hand in welcome. "Golly, buddy, I just can't tell you how glad I am to see you."

Abbrodani grunted and waved the man away.

"No, really, you've got to believe me, pal. I know less about this whole crazy thing than you do. Here, wait a second. I'll show you."

With a hand on Abbrodani's shoulder, he fumbled inside his jacket pocket. "I know I've got it somewhere. . . . Gee, I was so relieved to see your face, I almost wet my pants. Here. Look here. What'd I say, right?"

And with a chuckle and a wink and a squeeze on Abbrodani's shoulder, Orville Peabody pulled out the Swiss Army knife he had carried since he was ten years old and slashed open the man's throat.

ROME (AP) Diplomatic tensions mount as the mystery surrounding the violent deaths of three international terrorists remains unsolved.

Franco Abbrodani, suspected leader of the Italian Red Army Underground, Hans Bofschel, head of the Stuessen/Holfigse gang in Berlin, and Miramir Quanoosa of the Arab Brigades, a violent splinter faction of the PLO, were all murdered at exactly 3:45 P.M. yesterday in different parts of the world and in full view of hundreds of witnesses.

The assassins, all dead, were identified as Eric Groot (Quanoosa), a clerk in a records office in Amsterdam; Pascal Soronzo (Bofschel), an Argentinian sheep rancher; and an American, Orville Peabody (Abbrodani), a clothing salesman from West Mahomset, Ohio.

None of the assassins was known to have any political affiliations.

Groot and Soronzo both died of cyanide poisoning, which was probably self-inflicted, according to medical examiners. Peabody was beaten near death by the angry mob who witnessed the assassination of Abbrodani, and was taken by ambulance to St. Peter's hospital in Rome. He was pronounced dead on arrival.

According to a paramedic on duty in the ambulance, Peabody's last word was "Abraxas."

In response to the mounting allegations between the PLO, Israel, Germany, Italy, Argentina, the Netherlands, the Soviet Union, and the United States regarding what power lay behind the extremely well-organized assassinations, the U.S. State Department stated that the president himself was looking into the source.

Of the American assassin's last word, "Abraxas," the department declined further comment.

The woman laughed as she tossed the newspaper onto the long redwood conference table strewn with other newspapers from around the world. Each held a front page story about the assassinations, along with pictures of the three assassins.

She was alone in the room. Sunlight streamed through the large windows onto the desk and caught the brown-gold wisps of hair that danced around her face. It was a beautiful face, strong and elegant, but marred by a long scar that ran from one temple diagonally toward her chin. It missed her eye and mouth by a half-inch, so the features were not distorted; still, it was an unsettling face, a face that commanded attention. From the woman's imperial stance and the calm manner of her hands, it was clear she knew it.

"It's working," she said, lighting a cigarette. The casual remark was directed toward a camera propped in a corner of the ceiling. It buzzed faintly in the quiet enclosure, focusing on the newspaper the woman had tossed in front of it.

"Yes." The voice, rich and modulated, came from several sources at once. The speakers were mounted unobtrusively inside the walls, and when the voice spoke, it seemed to surround the empty table. "Excellent, Circe. A true success. Even to the American's dying word."

"Abraxas," she said softly, the word forming through a cloud of white tobacco smoke.

The tone of the voice from the walls changed. "But this is only the beginning. There is still much to be done. At the conference we will begin our real work. The conference, I trust, is ready to convene?"

"Nearly," Circe answered. "We have had some difficulty in locating one of the delegates. But he has been found. He will be approached today."

"Which one?"

"The computer expert," she said, squinting through the smoke into the sunlight. "The one named Smith. Harold W. Smith, of Folcroft Sanitarium in Rye, New York."

Chapter Two

His name was Remo and he was on fire. The flames lapped up his back, disintegrating his shirt as he leaped from one burning building to another.

They were tenements, crumbling, flat-topped monoliths in New York's South Bronx, where the streets were awash with smoldering garbage and sang with the wild shrieks of rats and frightened children. Remo hit the second building's roof, rolled onto his back to extinguish the fire, then without missing stride proceeded onto the third building in the blazing row. Mixed with the stench of burning mattresses and the insulation that smoldered in black columns around him, his fine senses could also pick out the smell of his own singed hair and the sickening odor of charred flesh.

He had been able to empty the buildings. Most of the people inside had made it to what shelter lay in the streets. The lucky ones would spend the night in a hospital. For the uninjured, though, only the night with its gangs and murderers and rapists remained. The arsonist had seen to it that a lot of people would get turned into prey for the city's predators this night.

In the distance, a siren wailed in place, stuck in the hopeless traffic. By the time the fire engines arrived, and the police, the fire would be out of control and the arsonist long gone.

He heard a sound. In the roar of the flames licking up to the roof of the third building and the noise of the displaced tenants and onlookers below, it was hard to make it out.

He pitched his hearing lower. Control of his senses was one of the first things Remo had learned in his long apprenticeship with the old Oriental who had taught him, nearly against Remo's will, the secrets of an extraordinary physical power.

It had begun more than a decade before, when Remo was a young policeman charged with a crime he didn't commit and sentenced to die in an electric chair that didn't work. It had all been arranged by a secret government organization designed to fight crime the way criminals fought crime—without rules. CURE operated outside the Constitution of the United States in order to protect that same document.

There were no armies in CURE. Only the president of the United States knew of it, along with two other men: Remo, the enforcer arm of the organization, and CURE's director, Dr. Harold W. Smith, a bespectacled, middle-aged man who ran the operation from a bank of the most powerful secret computers in the world. It was Smith who had arranged, so long ago, for Remo's transformation at the hands of the old Korean master, Chiun, into the most effective killing machine ever employed by a modern nation. It was Smith, in fact, who had created a master assassin from a dead man.

Nothing of that dead policeman existed anymore except for the veneer of Remo's appearance: the slim body, unusual only because of its extraordinarily thick wrists, the dark hair, the eyes some women described as cruel, and the mouth others called kind. The rest of him was a product of more than a decade's training and patience and work.

The old Remo had feared fire with the primordial, irrational terror born into the human species. The new Remo, this Remo on the burning buildings, feared nothing.

It was part of the peace that came with being a dead man.

He listened. The sound was faint but clear, a small voice calling out from below the tarpaper roof.

"Is someone there?" It was like the mewling of a cat, so small, so frightened. He had missed one. There was a child inside. Remo's heart hammered.

His movements were instinctive. Whirling to the edge of the roof, he placed his hands on one of the bricks making up the small safety skirt. It was already greasy with soot, and smoke crawled up the sides of the building like moving shadows, pouring into his lungs. He slowed his breathing, so that he would take in as little air as possible, then began a rapid drum on the brick. His fingers moved so fast, they were no more than a blur. A high sound, like a whistle, emanated from the wall for a moment, and then the brick broke off, shaped in a perfect wedge with a razor-sharp cutting edge.

"Please, somebody, help."

He was operating at peak now. His ears located the exact source of the voice, and Remo concentrated on the spot, focusing his whole body and mind on it, the wedge balanced easily in his right hand. Then, weighing his weapon, feeling its center and essence, he loosed the wedge of brick onto the tarpaper surface with a crack that split the air.

The brick sliced cleanly through the pebbled tarpaper, and below it, the wooden beams cracked as the roof split and gave. He smashed through the broken surface with one foot. After that, the roof gave way like a spiderweb, and he crawled in after the trapped child.

It was hot inside. The building, Remo knew, was ready to blow. The top floor hadn't yet been touched by the flames, but the heat had all but sucked out what oxygen there had been, and the smoke, coming in from every crack in the room, hung heavy as mist.

Enlarging his pupils to adjust instantly to the smoky darkness inside the building, he spotted what he was looking for. A bundle of rags lay in a corner, whimpering. "Help," it called again.

"Don't worry, sweetheart," Remo said gently, making his way toward the rags. "You'll be out of here in no time." He reached out his arms to encircle the trembling child. "You're safe now," he whispered. "You're safe."

"Safer than you." The voice inside the rags had changed in an instant to one of grating mockery, and in that same instant, a hand flashed out from the folds of filthy cloth. Remo caught the glint of metal as the switchblade sang, arcing, toward him.

Stunned, his reflexes performed the tasks his mind was too confused to follow. He drew back, feeling the whistle of the knife's wake against the skin on his throat. At the same time, one foot jutted upward to shatter the attacker's knife hand. As an extension of the same movement, his left arm swung around to meet the man's neck. It was a killing blow, as all of Remo's automatic moves were, and he watched the head bob once, almost delicately, before the eyes rolled white and the man slid to the floor. It was finished in milli-seconds.

Remo stood, waiting. The room was not empty; he had no need to turn around to know that others were behind him. For Remo, space was a palpable thing. Just as fish can sense the occupancy of their waters, so Remo knew that the silent room had three other people in it, and that those three had not come empty-handed. But there was no real movement from them, nothing but the usual sloppy motions of breathing and shifting weight that most human beings performed without even knowing it, so Remo waited. When they attacked, as he was sure they would, he would be ready. For the moment, though, he wanted to see the man he had killed.

He was young. The sparse beard on his chin was probably in its first growth. Out of the denim jacket he wore, covered with emblems and chrome studs, spilled several packs of matches. The jacket, indeed the whole room, smelled faintly of kerosene.

"Some fun, huh, kid?" Remo said absently to the corpse.

"Watch it. We got a gun," came the inevitable boast from behind him.

Remo turned slowly. He was relieved to see that the others were older than the dead boy. The one holding the pistol, their apparent leader, stepped forward, grinning and wielding the gun with the bravado of an amateur. He was ugly and muscular, and the grime on his face looked as if it had arrived there thirty years before and rested undisturbed since then. The gun in his hand was an old .22 Beretta, well used and discarded by its original owner, from the looks of it.

"We heard you nosing up there on the roof," he said, the arrogant smile baring an incomplete set of bad teeth. "You think you're Mr. Good Citizen or something?"

"Well, something anyway," Remo said.

"I got news for you, Mr. Good Citizen. This fire's ours."

"No kidding. I never would have guessed."

"This here fire's for the oppressed," put in one of the others stolidly.

"Yeah. Nobody should live in slums like this," said the third.

Outside, the fire engines and ambulances pulled to a halt, their sirens winding down to a low cry as the injured tenants screamed in relief and impatience. "You've done good," Remo said. "Now everybody can live on the street."

"Big deal," the leader said. "These buildings should have burned years ago. We just did those slobs down there a favor." His scowl turned into a grim smile. "Plus we got our rocks off. Right, boys?"

"Right," the two behind him agreed.

Smoke was pouring in from a crack in the far side of the ceiling, well away from the hole Remo had made when he entered. "Uh, listen, fellas . . ." he began.

"You listen, shithead!" the leader shouted.

Remo rolled his eyes. "Take your time, pal. But you might want to know that the roof's going to give." His eyes wandered back to the spot in the ceiling behind the men, where the smoke was jetting out in a thin black stream.

The leader smiled. "That's an old trick. There's nothing burning back there."

"I said the roof was going to give. The burning'll come after."

"How do you know?" asked one of the others.

"I can feel the vibrations from the beams," Remo said.

"Very funny. What do you take me for, a fool?"

Remo shrugged. "I wouldn't take you to a public trough."

17

"Shut up!" the leader yelled, his eyes glowing. "Now you listen and you listen good." He spoke with a whispered intensity. "Those cops down there are going to want somebody to pin this on. And it ain't going to be us, get it?"

"Heaven forbid," Remo said. "Then you wouldn't be free to start another fire down the street."

"You're catching on."

"The roof's going to give," Remo reminded him.

"Look, jerk, that roof crap didn't work before, and it's not going to work now, see?"

"Just trying to be Mr. Good Citizen."

"Well, you're going to get your chance, right, boys?"

"Yeah," one of the men said in a nasal twang as he stuffed his index finger into one nostril. "A chance to keep us out of jail." The three laughed uproariously.

"Here's what you do. First, we go up on the roof—"

"The roof won't be here in another thirty seconds," Remo said.

"The next roof, stupid. I got a can of kerosene all ready for you."

"Use it yourself," Remo said. "It's wonderful for cutting through grease and grime."

"Then Junior's going to kill you."

Junior swung a baseball bat from behind his back, grinning delightedly.

"Then we stick the can of kerosene in your hands and push you off. One dead arsonist for the pigs."

18

"Oh," Remo said. "I thought you wanted me to do something hard."

"Get over there," the leader said, shoving Remo toward the hole in the ceiling. "I'm going first. Then you, smart mouth, and don't try any funny stuff, 'cause Junior'll be right behind you."

"Junior's never going to make it," Remo said.

"The roof?"

Remo nodded.

"We'll take our chances," the leader said disgustedly, climbing out onto the roof.

Three seconds later the first section of the roof collapsed.

The leader scrambled clumsily to the edge as the screams of the trapped men died beneath the falling timber. He remained there for a moment, frozen, trying to decide whether to check on the others or run. He opted for running.

"They're all dead anyway," he muttered as he pulled himself across the gap of sky between one building and the next. The firemen below would be too busy battling the flames to chase after him. He could crawl down the fire escape and lose himself in the crowd of displaced tenants on the sidewalks. No one would catch on. And the bodies on the top floor would tell the story about who set the fires.

It was all worked out. He breathed easier as he brought himself to his knees on the roof containing the kerosene can. Just a few feet over to the fire escape . . .

"Hey, what about your friends?" called a voice

from the smoking wreckage behind him. It was the stranger with the thick wrists, pulling himself onto the edge of the building with one hand while he dragged something with the other.

"How'd you get out?" the arsonist choked, unbelieving.

"I flew. I have a wonderful body," Remo said, his hands busy. "Thanks to twelve minutes of pulse-raising exercise every other day."

"Wh-what about . . . ?" The leader edged toward the fire escape. "They alive?"

"No, they're dead," Remo said, flinging something out of the wreckage. It sailed high into the air, coming to rest with a heavy thump at the arsonist's feet, directly in front of the fire escape. It was the bodies of the two men, their limbs broken and knotted together.

"Real dead," Remo said. "And guess who's next."

The arsonist screamed.

Blubbering in fear, he pushed and pulled at the twisted mass of flesh in front of him to clear the way for his escape. But the stranger with the thick wrists had crossed the roof in one easy stride and was practically on him now. The arsonist rolled away, his teeth bared. From his pocket he extracted a squat, dark object. With a snap, the blade shot upward and gleamed in the moonlight.

"Okay," he said hoarsely, his smile twitching. "You try and get me now." He circled Remo menacingly, the blade slashing.

"First things first," Remo said. He stepped over

the dead bodies and yanked up hard on the metal railings of the fire escape. It gave with a crash, bolts and shards flying as the stairway came loose and splintered to the ground. "Now, you were saying?"

The arsonist stared at him with eyes like saucers. "How'd you do that?" he cheeped.

"The same way I do this." Entering into a flying spiral, Remo left the surface of the roof in a movement that looked like a dance, except that the turns in his maneuver were fifty times faster than any dancer's. His foot shot out a full two feet away from the arsonist. Still, the knife soared, shattering in the air high above their heads. The arsonist stared at his empty hand in amazement, then at the empty place where the fire escape once stood.

"Nuh," the man blurted, rushing for Remo in a desperate tackle.

Remo picked up the kerosene can. "Catch." He tossed it in what looked like a slow underhand lob, but the impact of the can broke both the man's arms and shattered his ribs before propelling him toward the edge of the building.

"Don't kill me," the man wheezed as he tottered on the brick skirt of the roof, the kerosene can lodged in his chest.

"Now, why should I kill you?" Remo asked. He poked the can with two fingers. "Gravity's going to kill you." With that, the man careened over the edge and screamed his way to the pavement below.

"That's the biz, sweetheart," Remo said, looking absently for a way off the roof.

There was only one. Straight down.

He readied himself now. The back of the building faced onto a court of sorts, a jumble of debris surrounded by chicken wire. Still, it made a better surface than concrete if you were planning to make a fifty-foot dive and come out of it alive.

He balanced on the balls of his feet, preparing. When he was in perfect balance, the muscles relaxed, the spine loose and ready, the feet in position to spring, he jumped high and wide, somersaulting in the air.

He landed on the balls of his feet, in exactly the same position in which he had started. In front of the row of burning buildings, a team of ambulance paramedics was scraping the arsonist's remains off the sidewalk.

"Anything I can do?" Remo offered as he sauntered out of the alley between the buildings.

"No, thanks," the paramedic said, pushing the body into a plastic bag. "There's nothing anybody can do for the jumpers. People get scared in a fire, they jump, you know? They don't wait for the fire department."

"Maybe they don't feel like burning," Remo said.

"Jumping's just as bad. Every fire, there's a jumper. Somebody just said he saw another one."

"A jumper?"

"Yeah. Off the back."

Remo groaned. It was a policy of Harold Smith's

that anyone who could identify Remo and consequently compromise CURE had to be eliminated. Remo was tired. The last thing he was in the mood for was another death. "Okay," Remo said, scanning the crowd. "Where is he? What's he look like?"

"Old guy. Big thick glasses, can't see too good. He couldn't describe the jumper."

"Oh," Remo said, smiling.

"Don't matter, though. They all look the same after they jump." He pointed to the plastic bag. "Listen, in case you got any ideas, don't bother going back there to check. It'll just gross you out." He went back to slopping the arsonist's remains.

"Thanks for the advice," Remo said.

Chiun, master assassin of the ancient Korean House of Sinanju, was waiting for him in the motel room they shared in upper Manhattan. Remo walked in reeking of smoke. He discarded his tattered clothes in the garbage, then went to shower. Chiun was sitting in full lotus on his fragrant tatami mat in front of the television set as dramatic organ music blared into the room. When Remo came out of the shower, the old man was still in position, his eyes glued to the screen.

"Sorry I'm late. I was in a fire."

"Silence, odiferous one," Chiun said softly, his gaze unmoving. "Go bury those clothes. They smell as if you were in a fire."

"I was in a fire. I told you."

23

"Be still. I am concentrating on the beautiful drama unfolding before me." The picture on the television faded out with appropriately dramatic musical cascades, and was replaced by the bare hindquarters of two white infants.

Remo exhaled noisily. "Really, you'd think you'd get tired of watching 'As the Planet Revolves' after the first few hundred reruns. That soap's been off the air for five years. Rad Rex has got to be the oldest fag actor in Hollywood by now."

Chiun shot him a withering look. "I pay no heed to your disrespect. Who can expect respect from a fat white thing, anyway?"

"I am not fat."

The old man slid his eyes contemptuously up and down Remo's lean, hard frame. As usual, Remo unconsciously sucked in his stomach. "Fat," Chiun declared. "And stupid besides. Any fool could see I was not watching 'As the Planet Revolves.' It is a new drama, even more lovely."

The commercial faded into a picture of a teenager wearing a green surgeon's smock as he traipsed through a jungle wilderness. "Go do your exercises," Chiun said, staring fixedly at the television.

"Exercises? I just walked through four burning buildings."

"Next time run," Chiun said. "Running is recommended for obese persons."

The phone rang.

The connection crackled with the beeps and clicks of a telephone scrambler. These devices,

Remo knew, were standard equipment on all of Harold Smith's phones, including the portable one he carried in his briefcase.

"This is a secure line," the lemony voice said.

"What difference does that make?" Remo snapped testily. "You're still going to say everything in code, and I'm still going to have to meet you in some godforsaken place—"

"There's no time," Smith said. "Three international terrorists have been killed."

"I didn't do it," Remo said defensively.

"I know that. The assassins were all captured at the scene."

"Then what's the problem?"

"Haven't you read the newspapers?"

"I've been busy," Remo said.

Smith sighed. "The problem is that all three murders—in Rome, in Munich, and in Beirut—occurred at exactly the same time. It indicates an organizing force behind them."

"Sounds like whoever it was did the world a good turn."

"Not according to the international diplomatic community. The Soviet Union is blaming the United States for the murder in Rome, since the killer was an American. They say it was a CIA attempt to wipe out leftist influences in Italy. The PLO, naturally, is blaming Israel for the attack on Quanoosa in Beirut. Meanwhile, the Israelis think the Palestinians attacked their own man to make Israel look as if it's provoking another war. The man who killed the German gang leader was

Dutch, so now the Hollanders and the Germans are at each other's throat. . . . It just goes on and on," Smith said wearily. "What it comes down to is that nearly every military power in the world is angry about the assassinations."

"Even though the men who got assassinated were terrorists?" Remo asked, incredulous.

"The world of diplomacy has never been easy to understand."

"Neither is baby talk," Remo said. "Why are you bothering me with this crap?"

"Nothing will be resolved until whoever set up the killings is found," Smith said.

"What about the assassins? You said they were caught in the act."

"All dead," Smith said. "Even that was arranged. Two of them took cyanide. The third, an American, was beaten to death before the police got there. That's where I want you to start."

"At the cemetery? Now I communicate with the dead?"

"At the widow's house. CIA investigators picked one interesting fact out of this affair. It seems that not only did the assassinations occur at the same time, but the assassins each disappeared from their homes on the same day as well, exactly three weeks before the killings took place. They all left suddenly, with no luggage and—according to the CIA—no word to their families."

"Doesn't sound right," Remo said.

"Precisely. My thought is that the CIA's methods of questioning the widow might not have been effective. It tends to lack a certain . . ." He fumbled for the word.

"Intelligence," Remo offered.

"Finesse. Especially with women. If their husbands had told them that they'd decided to leave their homes and countries to do murder, it seems unlikely that the women would admit it to CIA interrogators. But perhaps to you . . ."

"I'll take care of it," Remo said. "What's the address?"

"Two twenty-one Bluebird Lane in West Mahomset, Ohio. The widow's name is Arlene Peabody. I've sent a package to you via special courier containing the American assassin's picture and biographical data. It should reach you soon. You can leave for West Mahomset in the morning."

"Is the picture recent?"

"The most recent. A tourist was taking pictures of the rally when Peabody killed the Italian terrorist. The police confiscated it, but I've got a copy. In color."

"That figures." Remo never questioned how Smith got his information anymore. It was always accurate, and that was all that mattered. "I'll see what I can dig up. Do I talk to the other widows next?"

"No," Smith said. "One's in Venezuela, and the other's in Amsterdam. If you pick up anything from Mrs. Peabody, we'll know where to go from there. And one other thing. Peabody's last word was 'Abraxas.' "

"A whatzis?"

"Abraxas. The CIA couldn't get anything out of Mrs. Peabody about it. Keep that in mind. Call me to report at 2100 hours tomorrow."

"What time is that?" Remo asked.

"Nine P.M.," Smith said.

"You'll be at the office at nine o'clock at night?"

"Of course," Smith said, and hung up.

Chapter Three

It had been a foolish question. Smith was always at his office at nine in the evening. As the director of Folcroft Sanitarium, he could leave anytime he wanted to, since the executive responsibilities of running a small nursing home were minimal. But as the head of CURE, there were not enough hours in the day. Were it not for the human requirements of food and rest and, once a week, asking his wife if she was happy, Harold Smith might never leave Folcroft at all.

As it was, there wasn't enough time for CURE's original function of monitoring and, if possible, eradicating legally untouchable crime in America. Since the organization's inception, though, CURE's scope had broadened considerably to include every manner of unsolvable global problem. These days, running CURE was a nightmare of endless vigilance and constant fatigue for the computer wizard who'd left a high-ranking post with the CIA to take on CURE for a United States president with an idea. The president was now long dead, but his idea, CURE, remained. And with each passing day, it grew. Smith sighed. There was no way to do the whole job right.

At eleven minutes past midnight, he shut down the four massive computers in his inner office, stuffed some last-minute printouts into his attaché case, and drove home.

It was a quiet, starry night in early spring, and in front of the Smiths' tidy frame house his wife's crocuses and daffodils had begun to sprout. He never noticed them. For Harold Smith, night was no more than a testament to the day's failure. Spring meant only that another season had passed, another year in which all of CURE's necessary work was not completed.

His wife had left food for him on the table: something cold and boiled and covered with tomato soup, Mrs. Smith's favorite sauce. Harold never complained. In the years before his wife discovered canned tomato soup, the meals, being visible, were even harder to face. Now, buried beneath the innocuous red smear, Mrs. Smith's meals at least resembled food of some kind, and since Harold was never one to be particular about the details of his personal life, he ate it.

The knock came just as Smith was finishing up his wife's cabbage-or-lentil tomato surprise, the green and white striped printouts spread on the table around his plate. He was already beginning to nod with sleep. The sharp rap at the kitchen door startled him alert.

The man at the door was a couple of inches above five feet tall and wore his hair parted in the middle and slicked down like two black patent leather squares on either side of his head.

"Dr. Smith?"

"Yes?"

"Dr. Harold W. Smith?"

"I told you, yes. What do you want at this hour?" He looked at his watch. It was 1:12 A.M. Smith stood blocking the doorway. If the man had a gun, Smith figured he at least had a chance of slamming the door before the man could draw and fire. But the little man didn't seem dangerous, and when he smiled, his face seemed to show something like relief.

"A thousand apologies, Dr. Smith. It has taken me some time to find you. I followed you from the sanitarium—"

"I beg your pardon?" Smith said, the annoyance in his voice making it sound even more lemony than usual. "You did what?"

"I followed you. Again, my apologies. There was no other way. I had to see you alone. The guard at Folcroft would not let me in."

"He has instructions," Smith said tersely.

"And so, I waited for . . ." His eyes strained to see past Smith into the house. "You are alone?"

"As alone as I need to be. State your business."

"Oh. Of course." The man was clearly nervous, his hands fluttering. "My name is Michael LePat, sir. I am here to deliver a message of the utmost importance to you—may I come in?"

Smith stared at him for a moment. He could

see by the fit of the man's suit jacket that he wasn't carrying a weapon. "I suppose so," he said. "For a moment."

"Thank you." LePat's hands fluttered gratefully as he slid into the opening Smith had made for him. "This will only take a moment, I assure you. But it is a matter of indescribable importance, in which your participation is crucial."

"Do you think you could be more specific?" Smith asked drily.

"I will try," LePat said, "although I cannot give you all of the particulars. Suffice it to say that the individual I represent is a person of immense wealth who seeks to use his fortune in a quest for the highest possible goal."

"Which is?"

The little man swallowed. "The betterment of mankind, Dr. Smith. My employer has devised a project that will forever eradicate war and hunger and dissatisfaction from the face of the earth."

"I see," Smith said. "Really, I think it's a little late in the day to be collecting contributions."

"Oh, no. My employer has more than enough funds for this project. What I have been sent to ask you is your personal participation in it. May I add that you will be in illustrious company," LePat said, smiling greasily. "My employer has sought out only the top intellects in the world to take part."

"Thank you, but I really haven't got the time for this—whatever it is. Please convey my regrets to your employer." He eased the little man toward the door.

"May I leave a card with you, Dr. Smith? In case you change your mind?"

"I won't change my mind."

"Nevertheless . . ." He drew a business card from his vest. On it was scrawled a telephone number. LePat's sweating palms smeared the ink. "That's 555-8000," he said. "It's a local number. Just call it if you decide to participate in the project. Rest assured that nothing harmful or distasteful will come to you."

"I understand," Smith said, pushing the man out the door.

"You'll receive further instructions over the telephone."

"Indeed. Good night." He pressed against the door until the lock snapped in place, then threw the card in the wastepaper basket.

At 7:43 A.M. Smith was back at the Folcroft computer console, listening to the soft hum of the powerful machines. If he'd had to, he probably would have admitted that he felt more comfortable here than in his own bed. The Folcroft Four, as he secretly addressed the great electronic brains, were a source of the most sublime sort of security to the fastidious Dr. Smith.

They never stumbled. They were virtually incapable of error. Smith had designed the astonishingly complex circuitry of the Folcroft Four himself, using data collected from the banks of the most modern and effective computers in the world, and programmed them with the intricate mathematical permutations that only a mind as gifted and disciplined as Smith's could have devised.

For Harold Smith, the Folcroft Four were not just computers. They were more than storehouses of facts accessible to anybody who knew how to push the buttons. The beauty of the Four was that they were secret. CURE's information banks, in addition to being the most complete in the world, were utterly unknown outside the walls of Smith's office. They contained so much knowledge that if all the facts programmed into their software were printed out on one sheet of paper, it would take a man more than five thousand years just to read it.

And it was all his. His alone. All the knowledge of all the ages of man lay encoded in those four machines, and Harold Smith alone possessed the key to it.

The thought was awesome.

"GOOD MORNING," he keyed in crisply, as he did every morning, and waited for the megaliths to return the greeting.

The Four hummed and buzzed and bleeped, and then the screen changed color from dark green to steel gray, preparing to transmit.

"DOCTOR SMITH. CALL 555-8000."

He gasped. It was the same number LePat had given him the night before.

"GOOD MORNING," he typed again.

"DOCTOR SMITH. CALL 555-8000," repeated the message.

He altered the mode. "CODE 041265124. TRANSMIT."

"DOCTOR SMITH. CALL 555-8000."

He was shaking. The sensation coursing through his body was the closest thing to rage he had ever felt. He took the machines back to their earliest, simplest memories.

"CODE 0641. GIVE 100 REAL NUMBERS IN BASE 10."

They clicked and whined. With the tack-tack of paper processing, a sheet of printout paper spilled out onto Smith's desk.

"DOCTOR SMITH. CALL 555-8000. DOCTOR SMITH. CALL 555-8000. DOCTOR . . ."

Smith turned off the console. His palms were clammy. Someone had done the impossible. That greasy little man in his kitchen, or whoever he worked for, had invaded the absolute privacy of the Folcroft computers.

A shot of real fear pumped through his blood. If someone had tapped into the computers, then CURE was compromised. Totally. Anyone with access to the CURE banks would know the most secret workings of the U.S. government, including the illegal existence of CURE itself.

It was the end. That was the arrangement, made long ago with the first president who had found the need for an organization like CURE. It had to be secret, or it couldn't be permitted to exist.

And neither could Smith.

In the basement of Folcroft Sanitarium was a coffin. Inside the coffin were two cyanide capsules. They were for him. The computers themselves had been programmed with two sets of instructions to self-destruct. The first could be activated by the president's voice, in the event of Smith's death. The second was a series of codes to be operated by Smith alone, should the existence of CURE become known. Within seconds, fire generated inside the computers themselves would burn everything in the asbestos-lined room to cinders. No other part of the sanitarium would be touched, but Smith's office and everything in it would be utterly destroyed. That was the moment when Smith would walk down the basement stairs and close the door behind him.

"All right," he said softly. The time had come.

His attorney possessed a sealed letter to Smith's wife containing what little explanation—and love—he could offer his family. After more than thirty years of marriage, he would have felt like a cheat saying good-bye to Irma over the telephone, anyway. His daughter was grown; she could take care of herself. Remo and Chiun would find what peace they could. There was nothing left to do now but set in motion the code series that would blow CURE out of existence.

He pressed the numbers encoding the destruct orders and waited for the series to be verified on the screen. It would be the final transmission of the Folcroft Four.

Smith waited for the machines to begin, drinking in their mechanical noises as if they were a lover's words. The screen changed color. And on it appeared: "DOCTOR SMITH. CALL 555-8000."

He stared at it in disbelief. Every single function of the computers, including the self-destruct mechanism, had been overridden by one directive from outside.

Clenching his teeth, he dialed the number.

"This is a recording," the tiny computer voice on the other end of the line said.

"Oh, for God's sake . . ."

"Thank you for your interest in this worthwhile project. Your participation will help to serve the highest ends of humanity. Be assured that nothing harmful or distasteful to you will occur as a result of your willingness to further the future of mankind."

"Do get on with it," Smith muttered. He had already been through the sales pitch.

"Listen carefully, Dr. Smith."

He blinked, staring at the receiver.

"Are you listening?"

"Y-yes," he murmured.

"You are to go directly to Sandley Airport, twelve miles due southwest from your present location. A charter plane bearing the registration TL-516 will take you to a destination where you will receive further instructions. Please note this information, as your call will not be accepted a second time. That is Sandley Airport, twelve miles due southwest."

Smith jotted down the information.

"By car, your traveling time should be approximately 14.6 minutes. The timetable for your journey has been activated by this telephone call. In exactly eighteen minutes, the plane bearing the registration number TL-516 will be airborne. If you are not present on the craft at that time, the functions of your computer will not be restored. Also, you are strongly advised not to reveal your agreement to participate in this project, as we cannot be responsible for any harm that may come to those not specifically invited. We hope we make ourselves perfectly clear, Dr. Smith."

There was a short pause, followed by a beep. "You have seventeen minutes. Have a pleasant trip." The line went dead.

He clicked the cradle buttons. There was nothing, not even a dial tone. He pressed the intercom connecting him with his secretary. It, too, was dead.

"Mrs. Mikulka, are your phones working?" he called from the doorway.

"No, sir," came the unruffled reply. "All of the lines have been dead since I arrived."

"But I made a call."

"Yes, sir. Quite peculiar. Shall I walk to a pay phone and call the telephone company?"

He checked his watch. Sixteen minutes left.

"Sir?"

"Er . . . whatever you think," he said absently.

Well, he thought, he didn't have much choice in the matter now. If he were killed, the president's voice could still activate the self-destruct mechanism. That was on a separate circuit. But before he died, he would find out who had broken into the Folcroft computer banks—and how.

One other thing tugged at the back of his mind. The recording on the phone—so accurate, so organized—had said, quite clearly, that if he wasn't on the plane in time, his computer would not regain function. *Computer,* in the singular. It may have been a simple error, but Smith doubted that whoever was behind this scheme made simple errors. What was more likely was that the organizing force was not fully aware of the Folcroft Four.

A small ray of hope sprang up in him. Memorizing the instructions he had written down, he stuffed the note into an envelope and sealed it.

"This is for a person named Remo," he said, handing it to Mrs. Mikulka on his way out.

"How do I reach him, Dr. Smith?"

"He'll reach you."

"How will I know him?"

"You'll know him." Smith said.

Chapter Four

TL-516 was a forty-year-old DC-3 piloted by a man who appeared to have a considerable drinking problem. Smith, sitting ramrod straight in the copilot's seat with his attaché case clutched over his lap, mentioned it as civilly as possible as the pilot slogged down two inches from a fifth of Jack Daniels.

"Don't worry about nothin'," the pilot said. He exhaled a breath that smelled as if it could launch the *Columbia.* "Drinking's not my problem."

"No?" Smith asked archly.

"Nope. *Not* drinking's the problem. Once I quit, I start getting the shakes. Anything can happen then. Nosedive, fly into a mountain, you name it."

"I see," Smith said, feeling faint.

"Long as I got some fuel in the old tank, though, we're fine." He patted his stomach and took another swig.

Smith eyed the level of the bottle's contents. At the rate the pilot was consuming it, emptiness was imminent and the shakes inevitable.

"How far are we going?" he asked, trying to sound casual.

"Near Miami," the pilot said proudly.

"Oh." It was almost a sob.

"Got another," the old man said with a wink. He reached under his seat and hoisted a second bottle aloft.

Smith permitted himself to exhale.

"Want a blast?"

"Er . . . a what?"

"A blast," the pilot said, louder.

"No, thank you."

"Do you good. From the looks of you, something's got you wound up tighter'n a popcorn fart. Why, when you—"

"Thank you for your concern," Smith said, cutting him off. "Do you know who I'm meeting?"

"Lear jet," the pilot said.

"Excuse me?"

"A Lear jet," the pilot shouted, annoyed. "Old turkey can't hear nothing."

Smith harumphed. "I meant, do you know the person I'm meeting," Smith explained.

"Why? Don't you know who you're going to see?"

"No."

"Well, then, why should I?"

"Who authorized you to make this flight?" Smith asked testily.

"Telephone."

Smith steeled himself. "Was there by any chance a person talking to you on the telephone?"

" 'Course there was. What do you think, phones

talk by themselves? It was the base operator down at the airport."

Smith continued doggedly. "And who called him?"

"How the hell do I know?" He poured the equivalent of four or five doubles down his throat, wiping his chin with the back of his hand. "Some woman. Got piles of money, I guess."

"A woman?"

"Can't hear nothing, can you?" the pilot screeched.

The Lear jet was waiting at the end of the landing strip. The place seemed oddly deserted for a good-sized airport.

"Home of the wackos," the pilot said cryptically as he touched down with a bone-shattering thud.

"I'm sure you'd know," Smith said.

The passenger door of the sleek little jet was open. Inside, in the captain's seat, sat a strikingly beautiful woman with a fragrant mane of long brown-gold hair.

"Welcome, Dr. Smith," she said. Her voice was as rich as velvet.

"The woman," Smith said quietly, remembering what the drunken pilot had said. "So you're behind this."

"Not exactly," she said with a faint Mediterranean accent. "My name is Circe." She turned to face him. The long scar on her face came as a shock.

"I recommend that you get used to my disfigurement," she said. "You'll be seeing quite a bit of me."

"I'd like to know where you're taking me."

"To Greater Abaco Island; in the Bahamas chain," she said. "A small white population, made up mostly of transient boaters. Sun, surf, and solitude."

"For how long?" Smith asked acidly.

The girl laughed. "Don't be afraid. You won't be held prisoner for long. A week, perhaps."

"May I ask the purpose of my visit?"

"I was hoping you would. Your presence is required at a conference to be attended by a hundred of the best minds in the world. You have been selected to represent the computer arts."

"There must be some mistake," Smith began.

"No mistake." She took a deep, bored breath. "In 1944, while on active duty in the OSS, you helped to design plans for a military data-storage machine that eventually became what is known as UNIVAC, the first computer. Since then, despite your obsessive quest for anonymity, the sporadic papers you wrote on every facet of computer operations from the earliest digital models to the first non-binomial language have made history. The fact that you received your doctorate after you were already established as a leading authority in your field came as no surprise to anyone aware of your abilities."

"How did you find that out?" Smith asked irritably.

"My employer has many resources at his disposal. Not the least of them is a tremendous supply of funds for research into our delegates' pasts."

Smith shifted uneasily in his seat. "That was a long time ago," he said, adding, "it was never my field in the first place."

She smiled. "Yes, of course. Your name has not come up in the literature of computer technology for more than a decade. You have never been employed as a computer analyst. You work as the director of Folcroft Sanitarium. Sure. And Bobby Fischer is a beach bum."

"What?"

She regarded him levelly. "The way one lives does not alter one's ability, Dr. Smith. Your *ability* with computers is what matters, not your job."

"You've got the wrong man," Smith said gruffly.

"We would if we hadn't traced you through a computer."

Smith stiffened.

"There's no need for paranoia. We assumed that if you were still active in the field, a computer would be near you. It was the best way to reach you. Your information banks weren't tapped, if that's what you're afraid of."

He felt as if he were going to lose control of his bladder. *The information banks weren't pirated.* He said only, "I don't believe you."

Circe shrugged. "That makes no difference to me. I just thought it would set your mind at rest to know that whatever arcane project you were working on wasn't snooped on. Not that we didn't try. Your circuitry is too complex. That was when we knew you were our man."

"But the messages . . ."

She cocked an eyebrow at him. "Think about it, Dr. Smith. The telephone."

His mouth opened as the realization hit him. "The phones were dead," he said in wonder.

"A general short-circuit. The emergency generator kept the lights and whatever hospital machinery you have operating automatically. The phones and the computer are linked, of course. They usually are."

"But the *message*."

"A special hookup into your phone system. Temporary. It's gone by now."

"And the recorded instructions to meet you?"

"A one-time routing. That line no longer exists."

He looked at her for a long moment. "You people are certainly going to a lot of trouble," he said.

"There's a lot at stake."

She didn't speak again until they touched down on a small runway on what appeared to be a deserted island. Tropical plants and exotic flowering trees grew along the strip in primitive abandon. But somehow the atmosphere of the place was strangely oppressive. The air was heavy with the moisture of salt spray. Overhead, a cloud blotted out the small, high sun, making Smith feel as if he were in an enclosed box.

Circe turned off the engine and motioned for him to leave the craft. As he rose, she folded her hand over the handle of his attaché case.

"You can't have that," Smith said.

"No?" She drew a pistol from under the seat and held it steady inches from his face. The gun was only a .22 caliber, but at point-blank range would have turned his face into a rosette garnish of flesh.

With a hiss of disgust, he left the case with her. "One more thing," he said. "When I asked you if you were behind this, you said, 'Not exactly.' Just who is your employer? Exactly."

She reached across him and flung open his door. The damp air rushed in and surrounded him like sticky hands.

"A name you may have heard of, Dr. Smith," she said, smiling slowly. "Welcome to the realm of Abraxas."

Chapter Five

"Abraxas, Abraxas."

Chiun stood on the small terrace of the motel in West Mahomset, a half-mile from the Peabody house, and muttered into the wind. His almond eyes were narrowed in concentration. His hands with their long taloned fingernails lay folded inside the sleeves of his long green satin robe. The breeze was high, causing the white wisps of hair on his head and chin to billow gently. "Abraxas," he repeated. "I am sure that is what it was."

"What'd you say, Little Father?" Remo shouted from inside. When the old man didn't answer, Remo peered out, stuffing the photograph of Orville Peabody into an envelope. "What's that?"

"Hmmmm? A name, I think. It is confusing." He shook his head. Long tendrils of mustache swayed from side to side.

"Tell me. Maybe I can help."

"Help? You?"

"Stranger things have happened," Remo said jauntily. "All right, then. Don't tell me."

"Abraxas," Chiun said, his face solemn.

"Abraxas?"

"That is the word. I do not yet know what it means."

Remo smiled. "Case solved, Chiun. 'Abraxas' is what this Peabody guy said before he died. You must have heard it on Cheeta Ching's Left Wing Propaganda Update."

"The news? You think so?"

"Of course. What else could it be? Smitty told me about it over the phone."

Chiun looked at once thoughtful and worried. "There is something strange about the name. I have difficulty banishing it from my thoughts. It seems to follow me, even in sleep."

"Abraxas? I never heard it before Smitty called."

"Is that so unusual?" Chiun snapped. "Most thoughts pass by your mind with no more impression than a butterfly's breath."

"That's Korean gratitude for you," Remo said. "I help you out, and you insult me."

"Another thing," the old Oriental said hesitantly, his pensive frown returning.

"About Abraxas? Or my feeble mind?"

"I *see* the name, rather than hear it. It is like a vision. And when I see it, the vision appears in both English and Korean."

"A vision with subtitles," Remo mused.

"Idiot. The name *is* the vision, the name itself! Oh, why was it my fate to teach a brainless white boy with the sensitivity of a buffalo?" He jumped up and down, the ancient eyes glinting with anger. "The name Abraxas is the vision. It appears in bold characters, strung on a webbing of fine gray lines—"

"Calm down, Little Father. I understand," Remo said softly.

"You do not understand. You are humoring me because you think I am an old man losing my grasp on reality. That is what the ignorant young always think of their elders when confronted with something beyond their knowledge."

Remo took a step backward. "Whatever you say."

"Silence! I should never have mentioned it to you. Go on about your business."

"Look, uh . . . I don't think my meeting with Mrs. Peabody is going to take long. Why don't you just wait here for me till I come back?"

"I shall do as I please," the old man said stubbornly.

"Sure, Chiun. I want you to. Really. It's just—"

Chiun clenched his jaw in exasperation. "I am not crazed, Remo."

"Okay, okay." He held the envelope in front of him like a shield.

"So? Will you please go? Or do you think that this doddering maniac will leap to the street to molest infants in your absence?"

"Aw, don't be antsy." He caught his breath. "I mean . . . I mean . . ."

"Never mind," Chiun said. "I am going to the library. When I return, you will see that the Master of Sinanju is still in full possession of his faculties and that you, once again, are wrong."

"What's at the library?"

"Knowledge," Chiun said flatly. "I intend to search out the lesser writings of Ung the poet and Wang the Greater, most important Master of Sinanju. If the name 'Abraxas' is of any importance, it will be found in their sublime thoughts."

"I don't know how many sublime thoughts are floating around the West Mahomset Public Library," Remo said.

"If it is a true vision, then it will be made clear to me."

Remo waited a moment longer, watching the old man. At last he said, "Okay, Chiun. I'll see you later," and left.

But the thought of his old teacher chasing after wild hallucinations frightened him and made him sad. He decided to call Smith as soon as he was through with Mrs. Peabody and request a leave for himself and Chiun in Sinanju. Seeing his home again would make the old man happy.

He walked to the Peabody house feeling very tired.

Arlene Peabody was a tidy little birdlike woman with a bubble of bright red teased hair surrounding her face and making her look like a sunburned medicine ball. "I just don't understand it!" she shrieked with an ease that led Remo to believe that shrieking was the woman's mode of communication. "I mean, he was right here, right *here* on the couch in his pajamas watching "Masterpiece Theatre" one night, and the next morning he was gone. Poof. It was like he vanished." She burst into a torrent of hysterical laughter followed by a heavy flow of tears.

"It's all right, Mrs. Peabody," Remo said placatingly, patting her shoulder.

She threw off his arm with a wild gesture. "It's *not* all right! Everything's a mess. The kids won't go to school anymore. People keep telling them their father was a killer. I can't show my face in the supermarket. The house is always crawling with cops and CIA men and reporters, and now you."

"I was a friend of Orville's," Remo lied.

"You were?" The tears were still fresh in her eyes.

"And I don't think he put himself up to that business in Rome."

She leapt up from the couch. "That's what I've been telling everybody!" she screeched. "Never a word, nothing. Just poof, gone. No good-bye kiss, nothing. He didn't even take a clean shirt. Then three weeks later he shows up dead. On the front page of the newspaper!" She wailed like a banshee.

"Mrs. Peabody—"

"Now they're saying Orville was some kind of political terrorist or something."

"The man he killed was a terrorist."

"Oh, who cares?" she stormed. "Orville and I hardly ever watched the news. He wasn't interested in that stuff. Cub Scouts and mowing the lawn, that was all Orville cared about. *Cub Scouts.* Is that a hobby for a killer? I tell you, he couldn't have done it."

'A hundred people saw him do it."

"I don't care. It must have been one of those clones or something."

"Oh, come on. . . ."

"Don't say it's not possible," she screamed. "I've got African violets that are cloned."

"I really don't think your husband was a clone," Remo said with as straight a face as possible.

"Then how'd he get to Italy? We have exactly six hundred and twenty-seven dollars in our savings account. It wasn't touched. Even if he'd taken out every cent, it wouldn't have been enough to fly over to Italy."

"He went by way of Newfoundland."

She looked puzzled. "Where's that?"

"Off the coast of Canada."

"That's stupid," Mrs. Peabody said. "Why would he fly to Canada to get to Italy?"

Remo shrugged. "Beats me."

"It wasn't him, I tell you."

"I've got a picture." He pulled out the photograph. It was a good clear shot that captured Peabody during the moment between his act of violence and his death at the hands of the angry mob. The man's face was radiant and unafraid, his eyes smiling with satisfaction.

Mrs. Peabody gasped and lunged for it. "This isn't Orville!" she shouted.

Remo looked at the photograph, alarmed. "Didn't you identify the body at the morgue?"

"Yes, but that was a clone, too. Look." She dashed around the room like a mad thing, picking photographs off the mantle and the end tables. She threw them at Remo. "See for yourself."

He studied them one at a time, comparing them with Smith's picture of the assassin. They were different, all right. The features were identical, but the bland, forgettable expressions on the faces in Mrs. Peabody's pictures of her husband bore no resemblance to the transfixed, almost mystical look of ecstasy in the photograph Remo had brought with him.

"He looks—I don't know—healthier or something in the new one," Remo said.

Mrs. Peabody made sputtering noises like a chicken gagging. "It was a clone, I tell you."

"Mrs. Peabody . . ."

"I know my husband's face. He didn't smile, for one thing. He said it gave him indigestion. And he didn't like the sun."

Remo looked up from the pictures. "What did you say?"

"He didn't like sun." She stared at him. "The clone has a suntan."

Remo slapped his forehead. Of course! That was the difference in the pictures. Mrs. Peabody's visual records of her husband showed a man who was not only sullen and lackluster, but pale as the underside of a trout. The "new" Peabody, however, the man who looked as if he was ready to pass out cigars after killing a man in cold blood, was dark. As dark as if he'd spent weeks in the sun.

"Now do you believe he was cloned?"

"I don't know what to believe," Remo said.

She sat down heavily. "At least you're honest," she said. "It's just too weird. But other things have been weird around here."

"Like what?"

"Like this Abraxas stuff," she said wearily. "That was what Orville was supposed to have said before he . . . before he . . ."

"I know. And?"

"And so that's probably why I keep thinking about it. I mean, the CIA was so interested in it and everything. They kept asking me what I knew about it."

"What'd you tell them?"

"Nothing. I don't even know what it means. Orville certainly never said anything about it. As far as I'm concerned, it's just some weird name. Only . . ." She looked at Remo through wide, frightened eyes.

"Only what?"

She looked away. "Oh, forget it. Maybe I'm losing my mind. I'm a housewife, you see." She whispered it as if it were a confession. "I've got problems coping, you know? I eat Valiums like M&M's. They probably softened my brain. I read somewhere that can happen."

"Only what, Mrs. Peabody?"

"I told my neighbor, and she laughed at me."

"I won't laugh," Remo said. He waited.

"Promise?"

"Promise."

"Well, okay." She looked at him sideways, suspiciously. "I knew the name before it was ever in the papers."

Remo felt the air press out of his lungs. "You mean Abraxas?" he asked softly.

She nodded. "It started happening right after Orville disappeared. This funny name would be swimming around in my head. You know, like a radio commercial that follows you around all day? That's what it's like. 'Abraxas, Abraxas, Abraxas,' " she droned. "I can see the word plain as day in front of my face right now. Oh, it's just weird."

Remo's face had drained of color. "Go on," he said woodenly.

"Don't you think I'm crazy?"

"No," Remo said.

"All right. The other night I was tucking my kids in bed as usual. It had been a really rough day, what with all the police and the CIA guys and the neighborhood hecklers and the newsmen and photographers and everything. I had to go to the morgue that day, too. It was awful."

"What *happened*, Mrs. Peabody?" Remo said impatiently.

"Well, it was just so rotten, I guess I went to pieces after dinner. I cried my eyes out, thinking about all kinds of things. Then I went up to kiss the boys good night. My youngest son was already asleep, but Timmy, my ten-year-old, was waiting up for me. He told me not to cry." Mrs. Peabody stared straight ahead, as if in a trance. "He said, 'Mommy, don't cry. *Abraxas is going to make it all better.*' That was the weirdest part of all."

Remo stood up. "I'd better go."

"You don't believe me, do you?"

"I told you I did," Remo said. "You're not crazy. You and your son aren't the only people who've seen that hallucination."

"It's not a hallucination!" she shrieked. "Abraxas is a *name*. He's somebody, a person. I tell you he cloned Orville, and God only knows what he's going to do to the rest of us."

"I'll check it out," Remo said.

The lady was nutty as a fruitcake. Still, something in her words made Remo shiver.

What, he asked himself on his way back to the motel. That the strange name, Abraxas, sprouting simultaneously in the minds of three people, belonged to a real person? Crazy. Simply crazy. It just wasn't possible.

God only knows what he's going to do to the rest of us.

Chapter Six

He owed Chiun an apology.

Remo walked back slowly, trying to make sense of the strange trail where Smith's simple assignment had led him. So far, he knew next to nothing: A man named Orville Peabody had disappeared from his home to emerge three weeks later as an international assassin. Judging from his tanned skin, Peabody had probably spent those weeks in a warm climate. But doing what? And for whom? What had accounted for the drastic change in his personality shown by the photographs?

Then there was the Abraxas connection. That was the most puzzling part of the whole business. A man's dying word, seen before the fact by his wife and mentioned again by his child. *Abraxas is going to make it all better,* the kid had said, if Remo was to believe Mrs. Peabody.

And he did believe her. What she had told him was too close to Chiun's description of his own visions to be tossed aside as lunacy.

It had been a mistake not to trust Chiun. Abraxas was the key to the riddle that had been woven like a net around the murders of the three terrorists, and Chiun was one of the people who held it.

"Little Father, I'm sorry," Remo began as he entered the motel room, but the words stuck in his throat at the sight that confronted him.

In the middle of the room stood a black lacquer edifice of some kind, trimmed in gold and reaching as high as the ceiling. It resembled a miniature stepped pyramid, like photographs Remo had seen of the ancient Aztec tombs at Chichen Itza. At each of its many levels burned long fragrant ivory-colored tapers that made the pryamid shimmer with bright flame.

"What the hell is that?" Remo asked, incredulous.

"A shrine," Chiun said blandly.

"Where'd you get it? It looks like a model of something."

"It was. I removed it from the library."

"You stole it?"

Chiun clucked. "How crass you are. The Master of Sinanju has no need to steal. I told them you would pay for it."

"Great. That's just great." Remo paced around the room. "What'd you take it for, anyway?"

"It was not being put to proper use. Some fool had covered it with signs calling it a tomb."

"Oh," Remo said. "And of course, anyone can see what this splendid object's real use is."

"Of course."

60

Remo exploded. "Then would you mind letting me in on the secret? Because it sure looks like a model of a tomb to me."

"Lout." The old man sniffed. "It is an object of worship. Obviously."

"To what?"

"To Abraxas." The old man's eyes sparkled.

"Oh, no."

"I have found the knowledge I was seeking." He floated into a full lotus in front of the pyramid.

Remo sat down beside him. "Okay, who's Abraxas?"

"I thought I was a madman in your estimation."

"I was wrong."

"Naturally."

"Other people have been seeing the same thing. I've got to know, Chiun."

The old Oriental smiled smugly. "Very well. I'll tell you. Abraxas was a deity worshipped by the ancient Chaldeans from between 1000 and 600 B.C., according to your calendar. His followers proclaimed him to be a god of both good and evil, light and darkness. Hence the white candles upon the black shrine."

"600 B.C.," Remo reflected, wondering how a forgotten god from a lost civilization could possibly figure into a ring of modern-day assassins. "That's *old*."

"Old enough to be of merit," Chiun said, conferring his highest praise upon the deity. "Perhaps Abraxas was an acquaintance of the great Wang himself."

"Did Wang say so?"

Chiun snorted in contempt. "Not one of the greatest Master's writings was included in the inferior collection of worthless books at the library," he said. "I had to command the librarian to seek the information about Abraxas through lesser channels."

"I can't figure this out."

Chiun patted his head sympathetically. "It is not the place of white men to understand." With a quick look to the balcony, the old man rose from the floor and dashed out. "It is time," he said hurriedly, checking the position of the sun.

"For what?"

"The Noon News, featuring the lovely Cheeta Ching."

"Come on," Remo whined. "This is serious. Can't you put off watching that fly-eating armadillo until the next newscast?"

"If you cannot bear the sight of such beauty as Cheeta Ching's, then leave. Go stare at ox-teated white women." He switched on the set.

With a sigh, Remo watched the screen dissolve onto the pancake-faced, fang-toothed visage of the Channel 3 anchorwoman.

"Good afternoon," Cheeta said through snarling lips. "There's a new wrinkle in the international fracas involving the assassination of three terrorists earlier this week. Small but vocal groups around the world are calling for the posthumous pardon of the three assassins who lost their lives after eliminating the known terrorists."

"Assassins," Chiun said with disgust. "They

use the word to mean any bumbling fool with a weapon. Even Mr. Pea Shooter."

"Peabody," Remo muttered.

"In Washington this morning, demonstrators rallied in front of the White House to demand that the government extend a formal apology and full restitution to the widow of Orville Peabody, who killed terrorist Franco Abbrodani in Rome last Monday. The demonstrators, calling the assassination an act of heroism, are being dispersed by Washington police for assembling without a permit."

The image shifted to a group of people picketing outside the White House gates as police attempted to break up the crowd.

"What is the purpose of this gathering?" an unseen reporter asked a burly working man in his forties.

"We want to clear the memory of Orville Peabody," he said. "Peabody was an agent of God. When he killed that Eyetalian troublemaker, he made the world better for all of us." Cheers went up behind him.

The screen switched back to Cheeta Ching. "What marks these worldwide demonstrations is a seeming lack of organizational leadership. When asked by authorities to produce their assembly permit, the Washington demonstrators stated that they were called together by an invisible force named Abraxas. Whether or not this is related to Mr. Peabody's famous last word is not known. Nor is the fascist Washington government's reaction to the demand. This is Cheeta Ching, the voice of truth. More news at six o'clock."

"Oh, God," Remo said. "I've got to call Smitty."

"A fine idea," Chiun said patronizingly, turning off the television. "Emperor Smith's mind is even weaker than your own. It will make you feel better."

"I keep telling you he's not an emperor, and besides—oh, never mind." He waited for a long time with the telephone receiver against his ear. He dialed again. Once again the direct line to Smith rang. And rang.

"What's going on?" Remo said aloud. The direct line was accessible to Smith anywhere. It connected with his desk at Folcroft, with Smith's home, in a room where Mrs. Smith was not permitted, even with the portable phone Smith carried in his attaché case. Just about the only place in the world the direct line didn't go was to Smith's secretary's desk. It was for Harold Smith alone, and Harold Smith always answered it. Always.

"Something's wrong," Remo said, slamming down the receiver. "We've got to get to Folcroft."

They chartered a helicopter on the roof of the Pan Am building. Smith was good about keeping Remo in ready cash. The money came in handy for emergencies, even though he had to explain the expenditures to the penurious Smith later.

Well, this was one expense even Smitty wasn't going to complain about, he thought as he climbed out of the helicopter. He made his way from the roof down the walls of Folcroft Sanitarium. Chiun was ahead of him, easing down the sheet-faced building as if it were a stepladder. Hand under hand, the old man crawled deftly toward the reflecting glass windows of Smith's inner office. With the long, iron-hard nail of his index finger, he outlined the window and pushed at it gently until it gave. He caught the glass as it fell and set it on the floor inside the office before he slipped silently in. Remo followed, acknowledging Chiun's work with a brief nod.

The office showed no signs of a struggle. The desk at the computer console was tidy as ever, its drawers locked. The wastebasket was empty. The closed door leading to the outer office didn't look as if it had been tampered with. If Smith had been abducted, Remo said to himself, it was the cleanest kidnapping on record.

There was nothing to show that Smith had even been there except for the short sheet of printout paper that hung from one of the computers. Remo walked noiselessly to it. Not that he would understand Smith's arcane computer jargon but . . .

"DOCTOR SMITH. CALL 555-8000. DOCTOR SMITH. CALL 555-8000. DOCTOR . . ."

Remo blinked at the paper in his hand. He read it again. "What is this?" he whispered.

Chiun asked a question with his eyes. Remo handed him the sheet and walked to the telephone. The old man restrained him, motioning to the door leading to the secretary's desk.

"It doesn't matter," Remo said. "The place is clean." He dialed 555-8000.

"The number you have reached is not in service," the recording announced. He slammed down the phone.

"Who's in there?" shrilled a woman's voice from behind the door. The lock jiggled with frightened, clumsy movements. Mrs. Mikulka opened it with a gasp and stood stock still in the doorway, her hand on her chest. "No one's allowed in here," she said hoarsely. "Who are you? What do you want?"

"My name is Remo. Where's Smitty?"

"Oh." The tightness went out of her voice. "Dr. Smith had to leave unexpectedly, but he left a message for you." With an uncertain glance at the removed window, she edged back toward the outer office. "Er . . . Follow me, please."

> *Sandley. 12 mi. S/E*
> *18 min. DC3 #TL 516.*

"What's this mean?" Remo said, scowling at the neat handwritten note. "What's Sandley?"

"An airport, sir," the secretary explained. "It's nearby. But Dr. Smith didn't say anything about—"

"Thanks," Remo said.

TL-516 was the only DC-3 at Sandley Airport. It was painted red, and it had enough dents and scratches on it to pass for a World War II bomber.

"Who flies that red plane?" Remo shouted as he burst into the flight office.

The two old men were playing cards. One was bald, drinking coffee out of a stained paper cup. The other was swigging bourbon straight from a near-empty bottle. His eyes were watery and unfocused. He set down the fifth with a thud and smeared his hand across his mouth. "I do," he said.

"That figures." Remo strolled toward the table.

The man with the coffee saw the look on Remo's face and rose hurriedly. "I got some book work to do, Ned," he said timidly as he edged away.

"Hey, I was winning," Ned said, raising the bottle to his lips.

Remo yanked it away. "Hold the poison till we talk. I'm looking for a man named Smith. Tall, fifties, metal-rimmed glasses, three-piece gray suit, a hat. You see him?"

The old pilot tapped his finger to his forehead. "Little tetched?"

Remo cleared his throat. "I guess some people might think so. Where'd you take him?"

"Clear Springs Airport, near Miami. About nine o'clock this morning."

"Was he alone?"

"Yep. Didn't even know what he was going there for." He chuckled. "Tetched. Didn't even know the girl who sent for him. A real rich bitch, too. Isn't that right, Bob?" He glanced blearily at the bald man behind the counter. Bob jumped at the sound of his name.

"What girl?" Remo asked.

"I got it all here in the books, sir," Bob said, twitching.

"You the base operator here?"

"Eee-yess," he said hesitantly. "You from the FAA?"

"No," Remo said, grabbing the log containing the day's flights. "Jane Smith? You believed that?"

"She called late last night. I figured maybe it was his daughter."

"Didn't you ask?"

The man straightened. "Mister, there's no regulation says I got to find out what their relationship is. Anybody sends over a private armed guard with five thousand dollars cash for a one-way flight to Florida, I ain't going to ask no personal questions." He slammed the log closed. After a moment, he added, "Nobody forced him to go. He come up by himself. And he wasn't on drugs or nothing, either, was he, Ned?"

"Wouldn't even take a shot of hooch," Ned said disgustedly.

"Where was the call made from?" Remo asked.

"Miami. Said she was meeting him there. She sounded real nice."

Remo turned back to the old pilot and watched as he belched and rocked back in his chair, the Jack Daniels drooling off his chin. "Who picked Smith up in Florida?" he demanded.

"How should I know?" the pilot answered crankily, hiccupping.

Remo jerked his thumb toward the drunk. "He the only pilot you got?"

"There's another guy coming in about four."

"I can't wait that long." He walked over to Ned and hefted him out of his chair. "Come on, Ace. We're heading south."

"Hey, you can't take him," Bob protested. "He's stone drunk."

Remo threw the roll of bills onto the counter. "Think that'll sober him up for your log?" He hoisted the pilot over his shoulder.

Ned was singing "The Yellow Rose of Texas" as he fumbled with the panel controls. "Fuel rich, thrust up," he mumbled between choruses.

"Who is this person who fouls my air with breath like hyena droppings?" Chiun demanded from the wing window seat.

"He's the pilot. He's going to fly the plane. If he can figure out how."

"Once again, your unerring judgment has taken control," Chiun said.

"Very funny. He'll be all right. They say flying's like riding a bicycle. You never forget."

"I'm sure *I* will never forget," Chiun said.

Remo ignored him. "Okay, Ned. You've got to get us to Clear Springs."

"No problem," Ned slurred. "Just keep the bottle handy. 'Less you want us to fly into a mountain." He laughed. They took off like a rocket.

The pilot squeezed at the air beside Remo's face. "Hand it over."

"Hand what over?"

"The bottle. You do have the bottle, don't you?" He looked out the window. The ground below them swam in a pleasant haze.

"What bottle?" Remo said.

Chapter Seven

Most of the hundred best brains in the world were blotto.

Smith observed that the South Shore of Abaco, separated from the rest of the island by a tall fence, appeared to exist solely for the purpose of hosting a round-the-clock party. Some of the guests were famous people from different walks of life. Smith recognized a noted woman anthropologist who was dancing a tarantella on the beach. A former United States secretary of state, wearing a T-shirt with "Shake Your Booties" emblazoned on the chest, chugged down a pitcher of some pink and apparently alcoholic beverage while the crowd around him clapped and cheered.

"Cocktail, sir?" offered a waiter in a white jacket. He held out a tray with a dozen champagne glasses filled with pink liquid.

"No, thank you," Smith said tightly. The waiter walked away.

"Aw, go ahead," the fat man with a pink ribbon

pinned to his collar prodded, slapping Smith on the back heartily. "Loosen up."

"I don't drink," Smith said.

"Hey, you're missing something," the man said. He tapped the rim of his own glass. The movement set him off balance, causing the contents to slosh over the side in a spill of pink foam. He leaned forward and whispered conspiratorially. "You know, this isn't any ordinary booze."

"I'm not surprised." Smith turned away, but the man followed him, huffing with drunken indignation.

"Maybe you don't know who you're talking to."

"That is correct," Smith said tersely. "I don't know, and I don't care."

"I'm Samuel P. Longtree," the man said with exaggerated dignity.

"I never heard of you."

The man stopped short, then laughed. "I didn't think you had. I'm a chemist. My brilliant career ended at the age of forty with my greatest discovery."

Smith sighed, knowing that Samuel P. Longtree wouldn't leave him alone until he took the bait. "Which was?" he asked wearily.

Longtree brightened. "This cocktail," he said, sipping his drink. "Cheers."

"Congratulations." Smith moved away.

"It's really quite remarkable. It affects the cortex of the brain so that a person's anxiety is all but eliminated. Imagine that—an instant cure for guilt, tension, performance anxiety, nervousness, apprehension, dread, fear—"

"And rational thought," Smith added.

"Ah, that's where you're wrong, my friend. The beauty of my concoction is that it leaves the drinker utterly lucid. You can perform the most complex and detailed mental tasks and still be flying higher than Betelgeuse. All it does is free you of your inhibitions."

Smith looked at him fully for the first time, his mind piecing together the information with what he knew about Peabody and the other two assassins. "Guilt, you said? No guilt?"

"Zero. Good-bye, mother-in-law. So long, lawnmower."

Smith inhaled deeply. "No guilt, no ethics, no morals . . ."

The man laughed. "Hey, who needs morals in Paradise? Only dirty minds need fig leaves."

"How long have you been here?"

"Who knows? Who cares?"

"Did you happen to see a man named Peabody here? He was possibly with two others." He described the dead American assassin.

The man thought for a moment before a glimmer of recognition came to his eyes. "I think so. Came from Ohio or someplace?"

"That's the one."

"Well, I didn't see much of him. I've been busy adapting the ingredients in my cocktail into other forms. Do you know that it can be snorted, smoked, or shot?" He smiled knowingly. "Just name your poison. Of course, the injectable form isn't quite right yet. It produces some unfortunate side effects at first. Unconsciousness, that sort of thing. But the smokable version is a gas. Hey, maybe you want a joint?"

"Absolutely not," Smith said, unnerved. "Who would have seen more of Peabody?"

The fat man shrugged. "I don't know. . . . Vehar, I guess. He's the ad man on my task force." He pointed proudly to the pink ribbon he wore. "Say, you aren't tagged."

"Tagged?"

"Your task force. Pink, blue, or gold?"

"I don't know what you're talking about."

"You're new here, aren't you? Well, you'll find out soon enough. The colored ribbons designate what group you're assigned to. Task forces, they call them. Each of the task forces works on one phase of the Great Plan."

"The Great Plan?" Smith repeated dryly.

"The Great Plan of Abraxas. In capital letters."

Smith was stunned. "He's here? Abraxas?"

"He, it . . . whatever Abraxas is, his spirit has devised the Great Plan, and we are its instruments," he said solemnly. He looked from side to side. "I think I got it right."

"And what is this . . . er . . . Great Plan?" Smith asked.

"No one knows it all. The Plan is too vast for the human mind to comprehend, even the superior minds gathered here. All we know is the phase covered by our task forces."

"What phase includes your cocktails?" Smith asked.

"I'm part of Phase One," Longtree said eagerly. "It's called Unity. The job of my task force is to establish Abraxas and his good works all over the world."

"And Vehar, the advertising man. You said he's part of that, too?"

"Oh, Vehar's the big honcho in Phase One. Your friend Peabody was his drone."

"His drone? Wasn't Peabody part of your group?"

Longtree scoffed. "Oh, no. Peabody was a nobody. Nobodies aren't invited here. Only the crème de la crème. That's you and me, friend." He winked. "Peabody and the other two guys were just part of Vehar's experiment."

"What was he experimenting with?"

"You'll have to ask him. That's Vehar over there, the tall guy. But whatever it was, you can be sure it was for the good of humanity. That's what the Great Plan of Abraxas is all about."

Smith whirled to face him. "I'll tell you what your Great Plan was all about. When Peabody and the other two men left here, they went out in the world and murdered people."

Longtree smiled indulgently, snatching a drink off a passing waiter. "Hey, maybe that was their thing, right? Don't be so uptight. Have a drink."

"Excuse me," Smith said stiffly and walked away.

He approached a handsome young man dressed in expensively tailored playclothes, who was holding forth in the middle of a group of adoring listeners sipping pink cocktails. "Are you Vehar?" he asked.

"Hey-hey-hey," the man greeted expansively, pumping Smith's hand. "Look who's here. How're you doing, Kemosabe? Remind me to give you the address of my tailor. How's the little woman?"

"Do you know me?" Smith asked, bewildered by the man's overwhelming friendliness.

"Don't I?"

"I don't know you," Smith said.

Vehar straightened, casting a sneer in Smith's direction. "Then get out of here. I can't have riffraff imposing on my time. Besides, your suit looks like you bought it with green stamps." There was sycophantic laughter all around.

"I want to talk to you about Orville Peabody."

"Peabody? What's a Peabody?" He tweaked a young woman's nipple to her squeals of delight.

"Your drone," Smith said flatly.

"Ah, yes. It would take one to know one." His words were received with gleeful appreciation.

"How did you get him to assassinate Franco Abbrodani?"

"My dear fellow," the ad man drawled, playing the crowd. "How you managed to find a place in this think tank is beyond me. Any individual with even a moderately interesting I.Q. could deduce that Mr. Peabody's mission was accomplished through the power of television."

"Television?"

"Plus a forger for his personal documents, of course. We certainly couldn't allow Peabody's

76

actions in Rome to be traced to this place, could we?" The crowd tittered.

"The medium is the message," Vehar pontificated. He was no longer directing his remarks to Smith. The faces in the group were rapt with attention. "Send out a series of ultra-short-wave directives long enough, and every person capable of receiving the message will follow your orders to the letter. Am I correct?"

"Whatever you say, baby," a woman agreed, staring hard at Vehar's fly.

"Subliminal communication," Smith mused.

He knew that years ago, in the early days of television, enterprising advertising executives had managed to tap into the subconscious minds of viewers by flashing commercial messages on the screen at speeds too fast to be converted into conscious thought. All the viewers knew was that the brand names of certain soft drinks and household goods kept swimming uncontrollably through their brains, urging them to buy products about which, often, they had no knowledge.

Subliminal advertising was touted, among industry "in" circles, as the wave of the future until some legislators, seeing its dangerous possibilities, outlawed the practice.

"That's against the law," Smith said quietly. The group surrounding Vehar roared with mirth.

"Mister, ah—"

"Smith."

"How appropriate," Vehar said, fingering the lapel of Smith's suit. "Allow me to enlighten you.

The law was devised for a society without a true leader. With such a leader, however, laws are unnecessary except to enforce that leader's plans."

"You're talking about a dictatorship."

"Abraxas is not a dictator," Vehar said hotly. "He is a being of supreme wisdom. And in his wisdom he saw that Franco Abbrondani and his kind were the pariahs of the human race, a cancer. I was the surgeon who removed that cancer. Peabody and the others were my tools."

"It still sounds like murder to me," Smith said.

" 'Murder' is only one way of looking at it. Those of superior intellect see many facets in the same stone." He smiled, the blinding, false smile of his calling.

"Who put you up to this?" Smith asked, expressionless. "Don't tell me you've never seen Abraxas, either."

"No one sees Abraxas until Abraxas decides to show himself."

"Then as far as I'm concerned, you're the murderer. And you'll be brought to trial."

"Excuse me, Dr. Smith," a woman said behind him. It was Circe, dressed in a flowing chiffon dress. Her hair hung in soft waves around her face, nearly hiding the long scar. "It's time for your task force to meet. Come with me, please."

"I will do no such thing. I demand to use a telephone."

She led him away as the group around Vehar exploded into laughter.

"Doctor, you can't have gotten a true picture of

Abraxas's work through Mr. Vehar," Circe plead-
ed. "He's a bright man, but, well, sometimes a
little tactless. I promise you that you'll come to
understand us better with a little time."

"I want my briefcase," Smith said stubbornly.

"It's in a safe place. But I can't return it to you
until you at least give the project a chance. Won't
you come to the meeting?"

Begrudgingly, Smith went with her to a large,
sprawling residence on the edge of the sea, surrounded by palm trees and brightly colored hibis-
cus flowers. The mansion was painted sea-blue,
and fairy-tale turrets rose steeply from its corners. Banisters of white gingerbread surrounded
the third floor. There were more than forty windows, many of them made of stained glass and
cut into strange patterns.

"The trident of Neptune," Smith said, looking
up at the peculiar old windows.

Circe smiled. "All the gods are here." She
pointed up to a small window near the cornice.
"There's the lightning bolt of Thor, the Norse
deity."

"Abraxas's companions, no doubt," Smith said
dryly.

The woman bristled. "Abraxas did not build the
house. It was here, waiting for him." She looked
at Smith, harmless and confused. And probably
afraid, she thought. She had been watching him
since his arrival. He was the only one of the
delegates to Abraxas's convention who had not
melted with the flattery of being chosen as among

the world's best minds. He was the only one who had refused the drinks and remained outside of the group. He was a misfit, and didn't even seem to mind.

Smith kept his own counsel. He did not crave the reassurance of others. Alone, among all of them, this ordinary, drab-looking man with the metal-rimmed glasses and the ridiculous hat possessed a sense of honor. He would be difficult, Circe knew; possibly dangerous. For this she respected him.

Her tone changed. "The house was built by slavers two hundred years ago," she said in her beautiful voice. "It's full of secret passageways where the original owners used to hide themselves from invading pirates." She laughed. "Or so the story goes."

A cockatoo screamed overhead, its white wings brilliant in the sun. Circe pinned a blue ribbon on Smith's lapel. "You're part of the Phase Two task force," she said smoothly.

Smith stared at the ribbon, then at the face of the woman with the disfigured face and the voice of a siren. "Is Circe your real name?" he asked.

"No." She hesitated. "It was given to me after I was grown."

"It's the name of a Greek enchantress," he said.

"I know. She lured sailors to her island by the beauty of her voice and turned them into swine." She smiled.

"Is that what you do here?"

The question was unexpected, and Circe looked up at him, hurt. "Of course not. You're perfectly safe here."

"As safe as Orville Peabody," he said quietly. She didn't answer.

Smith looked at the sky and wondered if Remo would act quickly enough to save his life, because there was no doubt about it now.

Abraxas would kill him.

Abraxas would kill them all.

Chapter Eight

There are no great mountain peaks along the air routes between New York state and Florida, a fact for which Remo was eternally grateful. Ned the pilot developed a bad case of the D.T.'s somewhere along the coast of South Carolina and had to be locked kicking and screaming in the small toilet.

"I think I've finally got this figured out," Remo said, flying a loop over Orlando.

"Stop thinking and set this flying gin mill down," Chiun advised.

"That part's easy. They'll talk me down from the control tower. I've seen it in movies." He checked the map. "We'd better start the descent." He pushed the wheel forward. The plane shrieked as it catapulted toward the earth. "Hey, what's that?"

"Death, I believe," Chiun said calmly. "Instant death."

"The engine's not running."

A muffled shout issued from the lavatory, fol-

83

lowed by wild pounding. "Let him out, will you, Chiun? I think Ned wants to talk."

"The engines are stalled!" the pilot screamed, bursting onto the flight deck. "Bring the nose up. The *nose!* Pull the steering column back!" He looked out the windscreen. Highways filled with automobiles spread out less than a hundred feet below. Ned fainted.

"Geez, but he gets excited," Remo said, yanking back the steering column. The engines sputtered to life as the plane climbed steeply. "See? Everything's under control. That's the airport ahead."

"Less talking," Chiun said.

Remo picked up the radio. "Hello? Hello? Can anybody hear me down there?"

"We read you," a voice crackled from the squawk box. "Identify yourself. Over."

"This is . . ." He craned his neck to see down the side of the craft. "TL-516."

There was a pause, followed by another crackle. "You are not authorized to land here, TL-516. Please proceed toward your destination. Over."

"Not authorized? This is an emergency. The pilot's out cold. I don't know how to land this thing."

"Repeat, you are not authorized to land here. Any attempt to land will be met with forcible resistance. Over."

Remo exhaled a puff of air. "How do you like that. They're not allowing me to land. I never heard of such a thing."

"I thought this was the easy part," Chiun said.

Remo grabbed the radio again. "Hey, maybe you guys didn't understand. . . ."

"You are not authorized to land here, TL-516. Over."

"And you go suck a cowpie," Remo shouted. "Over and out." He ripped the radio out of the control panel.

"Very mature."

"Ned. Wake up," Remo said, shaking the old pilot.

"Wazzat?"

"Get up here and land this plane."

Tears streamed out of Ned's eyes. His nose ran. "I can't," he wailed. "Got the shakes. Bugs all over the walls. Sweating like a pig. Blood turned to water. Can't breathe. Seeing stars. Heart palpitations," he itemized. "Loose bowels. Double vision. Muscle spasms. Reflex . . ."

Remo collared him and threw him into the seat. "Land this sucker or I'll break your skull."

"Well, since you put it that way." His hands, shaking like a bongo player's, reached for the controls. He cleared his throat. "Thanks, kid. I needed that," he said gruffly. "Almost lost it for a while, but a good pilot never forgets. Which runway do you want?"

"There's only one."

"Oh." There was a long silence. "Where is it?"

"Oh, brother. *That* way," Remo shouted, pointing straight ahead.

Ned squinted. "Just testing you, son. Flaps down . . ."

"The *flagpole,*" Remo yelled, gesturing to the

tall metal spike directly in front of them. "You're off the runway."

"How can I be off the runway?" Ned groaned. "I ain't even landed yet."

"And you never will," Chiun said prophetically. "I am leaving." With a kick, the airplane door burst outward with a whoosh of air, and Chiun was gone.

"Hey, how'd he—"

"You too," Remo said. He lifted the pilot out of the seat with one hand and carried him to the door. Outside, the flagpole grew larger by the millisecond, its top now invisible.

"Help!" Ned screamed. "It's comin' at us!"

"Geronimo."

Remo turned a somersault in the air and landed next to Chiun, in the soft cushion of a treetop, the trembling pilot still in his arms. Four seconds later the plane exploded in an inferno of flame and thunder.

When the flying scraps had settled to earth, Ned uncovered his head and stared in wonder at the flaming spectacle. Apparently, falling out of a flying airplane had done much to increase his sobriety.

"Well, kid," he said, elbowing Remo in the ribs, "you got to admit that was one hell of a landing."

"Just swell," Remo said.

The airport fire trucks and emergency equipment seemed to race out of nowhere, spraying the wreckage with carbon dioxide foam. They were new, Remo noticed. Also, the runway was in perfect condition. Three small planes were parked near the main hangar. They, too, were new and expensive looking, as was the building itself. Clear Springs had the newest, shiniest, richest airport Remo had ever seen.

Chiun walked over gracefully, snapping a loose thread on the sleeve of his gown. "At least I can breathe now," he said. "That thing that burned up smelled like a brewery."

"Better watch out," Ned said in warning. "Too much fresh air can kill you."

"And your breath would keep me alive?" Chiun snapped.

"Hey, do you notice something weird about this place?" Remo asked.

"A lot of things are weird about this place," Ned chimed in. "Every pilot in America knows Clear Springs is the home of the wackos."

"Wackos?"

"Fiends. Dope fiends. 'Bout all they do here is run drugs. Lots of money in it, I guess. Built the whole airport just for themselves."

"Doesn't the city have anything to say about that?"

"Damn fiends own the city, too. Leastwise, most of the banks and businesses. They bring the dope in here in their own planes, and then truck it off to the mob somewheres. No trouble with customs, no hassle with the mob, what they call the Cozy Nosy, either. Got it all sewn up. Won't even let no planes besides their own land here, 'ceptin' special cases."

"Like what? I'd consider a crash landing a special case."

"Not them. The only special case they know is made of paper and colored green. The lady who sent the Lear jet must have greased their palms good."

The flames had been squelched. Two men were standing near the fire truck, talking and gesturing toward the crisp-fried plane, while the others put the equipment away. Both men drew weapons as soon as they spotted Remo and the others.

"Who're you?" one of the men grunted as they approached the trio.

"We're the survivors from that wreck," Remo said.

"G'wan," one of the men said, waving his gun. "Nobody coulda come out of that crash alive."

"Would I lie to you?" Remo said amicably, kicking one pistol out of sight and crushing the other into gravel in his hands. "Now can the tough guy crap and take us to your books."

The man who had held the disintegrated gun looked at the pieces lying on the ground, then at his companion, and shrugged. "I'm not going to give you no trouble," he said, "but Big Ed don't let nobody see his books."

"Let's let Big Ed decide that."

Big Ed was a strapping middle-aged hippie with a mane of frizzy blond hair flowing down to the middle of his back like a Saxon warrior's. He was a giant, more than six and a half feet tall, with a crushed nose and the mien of a man who had eluded the law for decades.

He spoke only one word by way of greeting: "F-A-A?"

"No," Remo said. "P-I-S-S-E-D O-F-F. What's the idea of not letting us land?"

"This is a private airport," Ed growled.

"A Lear jet landed here this morning."

"What's it to you?"

"It picked up a passenger. I want to know where it took him."

"That's confidential information," Big Ed said. He whistled. From behind the counter appeared four Cubans who looked as if they spent their spare time pulverizing bowling balls with their teeth. "Boys, show this dude the door."

Remo moved toward the exit. "I can show myself the door." He turned toward the door, opened it, and tore if off its hinges. With one swing, the Cubans lay sprawled, unconscious on the floor. "This is the door. Now where are your records?"

Showing no trace of surprise, Big Ed pressed a button. A loud wail, like an air raid siren, sounded around the airport. Heavy footfalls rumbled toward them from all directions.

"Commandos," Ned said shakily, looking out the doorway.

Chiun sighed. "And all with boom shooters." With barely a movement, he knocked the old pilot to the floor. "Stay out of the way."

Ned crawled to a corner. He looked up at Big Ed meekly. "Don't suppose you got a bar around here."

The blond giant drew a German machine pistol from behind the counter.

"Didn't think so," Ned said.

The Cubans were coming to, one by one. "You do the outside," Remo said to Chiun. "I'll take care of Conan the Barbarian."

Big Ed snorted, the closest thing to a human response Remo had seen him manage. "You had your chance," he said, gesturing toward Remo with the weapon. The four Cubans advanced. One of them prepared for a roundhouse right in front of Remo. Another circled behind him. With perfect timing, the man behind him squeezed his arms around Remo while the other struck. Only at the moment of contact, the man behind Remo was squeezing dead air where Remo once was, and the one in front blasted his mighty blow directly into the face of his companion. The two others, scrambling in for the kill, found themselves suddenly in midair, hurtling through the windows at high speed.

The shooting began. Big Ed's auxiliary troops stationed outside the building opened fire as soon as they saw the Cubans fly out like two human cannonballs. The back wall filled up with plugs of spent ammunition as the bullets missed the frail figure of the old Oriental standing in the open doorway. He was a point-blank target, but still nothing could touch Chiun. He dodged each bullet with a movement so small and quick that it was impossible to follow. To the men firing from outside, the old man seemed to be absorbing the bullets like a foam rubber target, unhurt and unkillable.

When the firing stopped, Chiun went outside. There was a scream, and then the thud of bodies breaking. From the broken window, Remo could see the guards falling, in twos and threes and fours, as the Master of Sinanju went about his work.

"What the hell's going on here?" Big Ed muttered, thrusting the machine pistol in front of him. He opened up on Remo. The thin figure in the T-shirt seemed to feint once to the right, and then was transformed into a blur, walking forward slowly. The pistol clicked, its magazine empty. Not one bullet had come close enough to Remo to muss his hair.

"Couple of spooks," the blond man said. "That's some karma you two got, man."

"It comes from thinking good thoughts."

Ed threw the pistol and ducked out of sight behind the counter.

Remo caught it with one hand. "Okay. Party's over," he said, following him. "Now, where are the . . ."

There was no one there. Where the big blond man had stood, nothing remained but the black and white tiles of the floor. From the corner of the counter came a faint scratching sound. Remo turned toward the noise.

It was Ned, crawling along the floor. "Is the coast clear?"

"Oh, yeah," Remo said, disgusted. "It's clear, all right. The creep's disappeared."

"Thank the Lord." Ned spread out flat on the floor with a sigh of relief. "Hey," he said, lifting his head. He was rubbing something on the floor. He dug at it with his fingernails. Surprisingly, the tile lifted, along with six others. Ned pulled it upward. A large square panel came away, revealing a deep hole with steps leading down. "What do you know," the old pilot said. "A trapdoor. Something these dope wackos would put in, all right."

"Ned, you're a saint," Remo said. "Chiun! Over here."

Remo scrambled into the hole. Ned scurried in behind him. Above, Chiun speeded up his work with the few die-hards who remained to fight for their missing boss. Remo heard three more screams, then silence.

Chiun met them at the end of the passageway leading from the trapdoor to the open shore of the ocean. Docked a half-mile away was a glittering eighty-foot yacht, rising majestically out of the sea beside a bobbing dinghy. Its small outboard motor was still running.

"That's where he went," Remo said.

"And he's going to keep on going," Ned said. "That ship's pulling out."

He was right. The yacht was turning slowly, preparing to head out for open sea. "You'll never catch him now. Ain't no other boats here."

"My pupil and I do not require boats," Chiun said haughtily. With that, he was in the water, heading toward the yacht at porpoise speed as Ned watched in amazement.

"Why don't you get back and call the police," Remo suggested.

"The cops? After what I seen you do, I'm calling Ripley's Believe It or Not."

"Better make it the cops," Remo said. "By the way, don't bother mentioning my friend or me. We don't exist."

"Anything you say," Ned said, smiling. "Hope you get where you're going. If you ever want to fly anywhere, call me. I'm in the book."

Remo smiled once and then vanished below the water.

Moments later, they were on deck. Big Ed was at the helm, the wind streaming through his wild hair; he was oblivious to the silent approach of the two men behind him. All he knew was that, within a fraction of a second, the ocean stretching in front of him was replaced by a close-up view of Remo's face, inches away from his own, and that his windpipe had inexplicably ceased functioning.

"I can kill you, or I can let you live," Remo said. "What'll it be?"

Big Ed pointed to his throat.

"Talk?" Remo asked. Ed's blue lips opened and shut like a flounder's. His head slapped back and forth in a nod.

Remo kept his finger on the man's windpipe. "Where'd the Lear jet go?" He released the tension slightly.

"Abaco," the man gasped. "The Bahamas. About an hour east of Grand Bahama Island."

"Who was flying it?"

"A woman. Don't know her name. Had a big scar running down her face. That's all I know, honest. Look, take the boat. It's yours. Just don't kill me, okay?"

"That's a deal," Remo said. "Now, don't forget to go straight home." With a heave, he sent the man arcing high over the side of the ship and into the ocean with a splash like a fountain.

He slapped his forehead. "The dinghy! He can escape in the dinghy."

"That has been taken care of," Chiun said.

By the time Big Ed reached the small boat, the fist-sized hole in the bottom had let in enough water to submerge all but the rim. He swore once, and looked up in despair at the two figures on the deck of the yacht.

"You can make it to shore if you swim in a straight line," Remo called.

"The cops will help you ashore." He waved as the sodden blond turned away and began the long swim back to land.

The air crackled with the roar of a jet taking off. A few seconds later a small, sleek craft whistled overhead. It looped around and dipped low, buzzing just above the ship. The man in the pilot's seat saluted. It was Ned.

"Looks like he found a way home," Remo said.

Chiun nodded. "Let us hope we can say the same for Emperor Smith."

Chapter Nine

Greater Abaco Island, it turned out, was not appreciably larger than the Houston Astrodome. If it hadn't been for Chiun's relentless search for TV antennae, Big Ed's powerful boat would have passed it by in minutes. As it was, though, they arrived, with, Chiun estimated, plenty of time to catch the 3:00 P.M. airing of "Ways of Our Days."

"Quickly, a hotel," Chiun said restlessly to Remo. "Preferably with cable reception. Also a vibrating bed."

Remo looked around at the unpainted shacks appearing at infrequent intervals between stretches of rock and greenery. From the deep natural harbor where they'd left the yacht, they had made their way to a single-lane dirt road where chameleons scattered before their feet. This, it seemed, was the island's main thoroughfare.

"I don't think that's going to be so easy, Little Father," Remo said. "Besides, we don't have time for soap operas. Smitty's trapped here someplace."

"He who has no time for beauty is but half a person," Chiun said.

"And you won't need the vibrating bed, either. Wait a minute. Someone's coming."

Down the road, a tall black man was ambling gracefully toward them. When Remo jogged to meet him, the man's face lit up with a broad smile.

"You run too fast," he said amiably. " 'Round here, plenty of time for walking, taking things easy. That is the island way."

"I'm looking for someone," Remo said, glad that the only person he'd managed to find seemed to be a cooperative fellow.

"Yes? Maybe I know him. Abaco is a small place. Most folks know each other. 'Cept for South Shore, of course."

"Who's at South Shore?"

The black man chuckled. "Nobody you want to know. They put up the big fence, nobody can come in. The folks there, they stay inside the fence alla time."

"Doing what?"

The man stuck his thumb in his mouth and threw his head back. "Drinking." His eyes twinkled mischievously.

"Oh," Remo said. "Well, Smith's not there."

"Your friend's name is Smith?" He beamed. "I know Smith."

"You do?"

"Naturally. Everybody here know Smith. Fat man, very sweaty, girls on him alla time?"

"Wrong Smith," Remo said. "This Smith is tall,

gray haired, but he wears a hat ... Actually, he's pretty ordinary looking," he mused half to himself. "But he might be with someone. A woman."

"White woman?"

"I think so. All I know about her is that she has a scar on her face. A big one, I guess, running down the side ... What's the matter?"

The smile had faded from the man's face. He backed off, making the sign against evil with his fingers.

"Do you know her?"

"I don't know nothing," the man said. "I don't see nothing. The South Shore not my business, okay?" He turned so quickly that he skidded on the dirt surface of the road, then headed at break-neck speed into the thick foliage of the hills.

"Your charm has worked its usual magic, I see," Chiun said as Remo walked back.

"I don't understand it. I just mentioned the woman with the scar, and he went berserk. But he said something about a place called South Shore. It doesn't sound like Smitty's kind of place, but if he was kidnapped, he might be there."

"It is as easy to walk south as north in this place," Chiun said glumly.

He was ecstatic by the time they'd walked a mile. South led into the village of Abaco, comprised of a grocery, a hardware store, and the Greater Abaco Beach Hotel, providing six rooms complete with television.

"Twenty minutes to spare," Chiun said, checking the sun. "Go and check us in at once."

"Come on, Chiun. What about Smitty? What about the way that guy freaked out when I mentioned the woman with the scar? Aren't you even interested?"

"I am interested in whether or not Dr. Sinclair knows that the wealthy widow he has just treated for manic depression is his long lost daughter," he said angrily. "Besides, you want scar-faced white girls? Bring her along."

"Who?"

"In the car," Chiun said impatiently.

Although there were only two automobiles on the road, a major traffic jam was in progress. One of the vehicles was a battered Land Rover, parked and empty in the middle of the street. The other was a white Opel, driving up onto the turf to pass the first car. Remo squinted through the bright sunlight to catch a glimpse of its driver.

It was a woman. With a long scar on the side of her face.

"How could you see that from here?" Remo asked.

"How couldn't you?" Chiun said, equally astonished.

"It doesn't matter. I've got to stop her." He ran toward the car, which had passed the blockage and was speeding up the road.

Chiun sighed and picked up a small stone. "The brain of a tuna," he said resignedly. He cast the stone.

It spun through the air with a sound like a whip cracking. A split second later the Opel's right rear tire burst and flattened, and the car shimmied to a halt.

Remo stopped short. He turned back to Chiun. "Thanks, Little Father," he said sheepishly. "I should have thought of that."

"The hotel," Chiun reminded him.

"Um . . . do you think you could register us?"

"I? I do one favor for you and suddenly the Master of Sinanju is reduced to servant's work?"

"Then just wait inside for me," Remo said, looking back quickly at the girl. She had gotten out of the car and was looking hopelessly at the blown-out tire. "You know how it is," he said confidently. "Women are my specialty. I figure if I can have a few minutes alone with her, she'll lead us to Smitty."

"Such is the power of your sex appeal?" Chiun's face was bored.

"Something like that. Just leave it to me." He swaggered off toward the car.

"Hi. Need some help?" He gave her his most winning smile.

She returned it. Point one, Remo said to himself, taking in the woman's face. She was a real beauty, all right. If anything, the scar made her look more interesting.

"You're staring," she said. The deep sultriness of her voice pulled him out of his reverie.

"I'm sorry."

"It's all right. I'm used to it. And yes, I accept your kind offer." The accent was subtle and hard to place. She opened the trunk, and Remo lifted out the jack and the spare tire.

"Do you live here?" he asked, hoping for a clue as to her origins.

"Sometimes. But you don't. I've never seen you before. A tourist?"

"I guess you could say that."

"A rare breed in these parts."

Remo jacked up the car and removed the tire, going slowly enough to give him the time he needed. "Say, I've heard some stories about the South Shore here. I guess that's really a swinging place."

She hesitated. "I'm afraid you are mistaken," she said cautiously, the rich voice losing its cheer.

"Oh, I heard it was pretty wild. Lots of parties—"

"I'll finish that," she said, reaching for the tire iron. Remo held it away from her.

"C'mon. What kind of gentleman would I be if I didn't finish the job? Why, just the other day I was telling my friend Harry Smith . . ."

He saw her stiffen. "Oh, do you know him?" he asked casually. "He travels a lot. Tall guy, gray hair but wears a hat—"

"I don't know him," she said harshly.

So Big Ed was telling the truth. The woman was going to lead him directly to Smith.

"Now, if you don't mind, I'm rather in a hurry," she said briskly.

"Almost finished." He placed the final lug nuts in place and stood up. "You know, I'm new here, and I'd really appreciate it if I could buy you a drink."

"I don't drink," she said.

"Then how about dinner?"

"It's three o'clock in the afternoon."

"An after-school snack?" He brushed her left wrist. She shivered.

Long ago the old Master had instructed Remo in the ancient arts of pleasuring women. It was one skill in which Remo excelled immediately. There were many ways of bringing a woman to ecstasy, but all of them began with the left wrist.

Plays like a harp, he thought. Scar or no, this was one seduction he was going to enjoy.

"I—I think not," she stammered.

In a seemingly accidental movement, he touched the outside of her thigh. "It would be a pleasure to see you," he whispered close to her ear. The small hairs at the nape of her neck stood on end. "A pleasure."

"Perhaps you had better finish with the tire," she said breathlessly. Her breasts swelled beneath the thin fabric of her dress. She was ready.

"And then?"

She brought her mouth to his. The sensation of her full lips pressing against him felt like electric velvet. "I'll wait for you in the car," she said.

"Yes, ma'am." Bingo. Five minutes, ten tops, and she'd tell him everything there was to know about Harold W. Smith. He stopped beside the jack.

All it took was a little finesse, he thought with some pride. She'd already started the car. This one was raring to go. He smiled as he removed the jack. Oh, well, when you had it, you had it. . . .

The car skidded away with a shriek of burning

rubber. Dust and soot plowed out behind it, leaving Remo in a foul-smelling cloud with the jack in his hand.

"Hey," he croaked through the pall as he watched the white Opel grow small on the road ahead. Hacking and wheezing for breath, he cleared two spots for his eyes from the greasy black film on his face.

"Ah. So that is how you work at your specialty," Chiun said, walking toward him. "I cannot tell you how honored I am to have been able to observe your prowess in action. The parting, I think, was most romantic."

"Drop it," Remo warned, throwing the jack to the road so hard that it disappeared beneath the surface.

"And now, perhaps, a little television?"

"Whatever you say."

Chapter Ten

The task force meeting lasted all day. Much of it was spent in lengthy introductions, the delegates pouring pink cocktails down their throats as each one rose to speak about his area of expertise. Smith's group consisted of a banker, a stockbroker, an economist, a military strategist, a mathematician, an educator, a historian, a journalist, an engineer, and the former secretary of state, who looked considerably more decorous than he had the last time Smith saw him. His "Shake Your Booties" T-shirt had given way to a white linen suit that hung shapelessly on his shapeless body.

Smith wondered about the peculiar collection of occupations designated for Phase Two of the Great Plan, but he said nothing. He was forced to attend the meeting, and he attended. Period. He would make no other contribution to Abraxas or his murdering council.

The man named LePat, seated at the head of the long redwood conference table, chaired the meeting. Behind him was a large blank projection screen. He was a changed man from the timid dormouse who had stood, hat in hand, at Smith's doorway in the middle of the night. Now an aura of confidence surrounded him. His manner was efficient and commanding.

The born bureaucrat, Smith mused, comfortable only when enmeshed in a net of rigid rules. Aside from LePat's mannerism of stroking his patent-leather hair, he seemed as much at ease as the imperturbable Circe, who sat on a corner divan near a film projector, smoking a cigarette.

Directly across from her was a television camera, humming as it swung in its continuous arc around the table.

"And, at last we come to the final delegate in the Phase Two task force, a man whose brilliance in the field of computer science will broach new horizons and forever benefit mankind in his work for the Great Plan of Abraxas," LePat said. "Gentlemen, I present to you Dr. Harold W. Smith. Please rise, Dr. Smith, and tell us about yourself and your views on the world and how we of the intelligentsia may improve it."

Polite applause sprang up, along with shouts for more of Samuel Longtree's pink firewater.

Smith remained seated. "Call the American embassy," he said directly into the camera. "I'm here against my will."

LePat sputtered. The camera stopped in its arc and rested on Smith. "But Dr. Smith—"

"Leave him alone," came a highly amplified voice from all four walls at once. The other delegates fell silent, searching the room for the source of the sound. LePat's mouth dropped open. After a moment, a whispered buzz of excitement circulated around the table.

"I am Abraxas," the voice declared, a deep, full bass sounding like a proclamation of Moses.

The whispers turned to gasps as the delegates clasped one another frenziedly and slogged down the pink cocktails. Only Smith was unimpressed. He folded his arms in front of his chest and continued to stare at the camera.

The voice answered his unspoken challenge. "Dr. Smith, do I detect some hostility from you toward our benevolent conference?"

"Oh, no," LePat said quickly, his veneer of self-control shattered.

"Let the doctor speak for himself."

Smith answered, his expression unchanging. "That is correct," he said. The room fell again to silence. Even Circe stubbed out her cigarette and sat upright, a wave of apprehension crossing her face. "The 'benevolence' of this so-called conference is a farce. I have been brought here against my will and my personal belongings have been taken by force. That, as far as I'm concerned, is kidnapping and theft. I don't know what sort of brainwashing you're carrying on here with your pink drinks and subliminal suggestions to do murder, but you're not going to make an Orville Peabody out of me."

The room burst into chaos. Shouts rose up from the delegates. The Belgian economist sitting next to Smith jumped up and lunged for him.

"You can't talk that way to Abraxas," he shouted, grabbing Smith by the collar.

A high whistle pierced the din and silenced it. "Gentlemen," the deep voice said, unruffled. The economist released Smith and took his seat along with the other delegates.

"Dr. Smith's reservations are well taken." The camera moved from its focus on him and resumed its wide, sweeping arc. At the doorway, where she had stationed herself in case of an emergency, Circe breathed a sigh of relief and walked back to her place on the divan.

"You have all been patient these many days, waiting while our assembly has gathered from around the world. During this time little has been revealed to you about the true work of this conference. I am speaking with you now to elucidate those plans so that we may begin together, as we will end, in a unity and harmony and peace that will spread to the four corners of the earth."

"Then start with how you turned Peabody and the other two innocent men into assassins," Smith said.

"That was not the case, as you will come to understand," the voice said calmly. More pitchers of the pink beverage were passed around. Smith pushed his glass away with disdain.

"For all the ages of man, war and self-interest have destroyed any possible cooperation between the peoples of the world. Where great progress might have been made, the ends of mankind have constantly been thwarted by petty provocations. I wish to see this unhappy state ended once and for all, so that the true potential of the human race may be realized."

Smith stifled a yawn.

"My plan to accomplish this has been divided into three parts: Unity, Harmony, and Peace. Phase One of the Plan, Unity, will bring together the disparate elements of society under one common banner."

"Yours," Smith muttered under his breath.

"Yes, mine." The camera swept past him. "Abraxas will not harm those under his guidance. Mr. Peabody and the others were the beginning of Phase One, rooting out the sources of true evil in the world and making it a better place to live. Already people in every country are calling the elimination of the three terrorists a major step forward in the attainment of world peace. Some of the rotten flesh of the body of mankind has been cut away, and the instruments of surgery—Peabody, Groot, and Soronzo, have grown to the stature of legends."

"They are dead," Smith said levelly.

"Yes. And in death they have achieved immortality."

"It was a bone," Smith said. The eyes of the delegates shifted to him. Smith met them. "A bone thrown to the dogs. An empty gesture. The purpose of those killings could only have been to dupe whoever was on the receiving end of those subconscious television messages into believing that this Abraxas character is some sort of Lone Ranger, spreading good wherever he goes." He scanned the blank faces of the delegates. "Don't you understand? *Three terrorists*. It was nothing!"

"It was not even announced that the executions were my work," the voice on the loudspeaker said.

"Peabody announced it. In a way that made every journalist in the world pay attention."

The voice rumbled a low laugh. "Very well. I concede the point. The murders were committed to propagate the name of Abraxas. Are you satisfied, Smith?"

Smith sat down, bewildered. Abraxas had just admitted that his "benevolent conference" was a sham. And yet the faces around the table remained unchanged, staring up reverently at the camera.

It didn't make any difference to them, Smith realized with sickening clarity. Good or bad, saint or killer, Abraxas had taken their minds and swallowed them whole.

"Those men were trained to perform their tasks through the medium of television," the voice continued crisply. "As many of you know, they were instructed by subliminal messages transmitted through ordinary television programs. The same can be done on a larger scale, bringing the message of Abraxas to millions. World opinion can be swayed in a fraction of the time it would take through normal political or military channels. There will be no dissent."

"What are you talking about?" Smith asked, aghast.

"Don't be dull," Abraxas snapped. "I am talking about revolution. *Revolution*, Dr. Smith. In a short time this conference will formulate and carry out a worldwide revolution without spilling a drop of innocent blood."

Cheers went up from the table. Smith hung his head, feeling nauseated.

"That is Phase One. Phase Two, Harmony, will speed up the process even further. Gentlemen, we must be realistic. Although the masses will flock to the Plan of Abraxas, those wielding power and money will not easily give up their privileges for the good of society. For this reason, the private reserves of wealth must be taken from those who hoard it and redistributed to best serve the ends of humanity as a whole."

Smith sat up with a jolt. "What?"

The voice continued, deep, hypnotic, assured. The delegates at the table listened in rapt attention. "The people in this room have been assembled to devise ways to topple the world's economy and remove the corruption of private wealth. Here in this room we will find a way to eradicate the reserves of the New York and American Stock Exchanges. We will manipulate, by controlling the vast networks of communications, the prices of oil and other wealth-producing commodities."

"I can redirect the telephone lines of the OPEC countries for a day," the Middle Eastern engineer cried enthusiastically. "Chaos for one day—it will be enough to confuse the world for months."

"I can have the mail of the United States monitored for an indefinite period," the former secretary of state announced. "All priority mail will be discarded."

"A beginning," Abraxas said. "And I'm sure that Monsieur Beaupère, our banker, can arrange for the dispersal of funds from large individual accounts in Swiss banks."

"Without a trace," the elegant Swiss said lazily, sipping his cocktail. "Some of the richest men in the world will become paupers overnight."

Abraxas continued, "And you, Dr. Smith. I would like for you to take on a project by yourself. Through your genius with computers, I want you to find access into the information banks of the Internal Revenue Service. You will feed false information into the IRS computers, and confiscate the funds handled by that organization. When you have completed your task, you will do the same for the tax systems of other nations."

Smith rose out of his seat in disbelief. "You're mad," he said in a whisper, not trusting his voice. "You're talking about the destruction of civilization."

"The *beginning* of civilization," Abraxas corrected. "Phase Three will be the culmination of all our efforts, the end to justify the means we will use. For Phase Three, Peace, is nothing less than the reorganization of the planet."

"War will be eradicated. Discord will not exist. Personal ambition and competition among men will be done away forever. In Phase Three, I offer you a world where each nation and all the people in it serve one function to benefit all mankind. Japan, for example, will be a completely techno- logical society, producing electronics for the entire world. All persons living in Japan will serve its one industry, and all will benefit."

"You can't be serious," Smith said. "Japan is a nation, not a company. You can't expect every single person in the entire country to work for one industry. What happens to everything else?"

"I'm glad that you're showing an interest, Dr. Smith. The Scandinavian countries will be the dairy center of the earth. Greenland, because of its geological stability, will contain the nuclear components to heat and light the planet for centuries to come. All of the fish and sea products used by the population of the earth will issue from a chain of islands in the South Pacific. The Soviet Union, because of its vast grasslands, will produce livestock."

"Livestock?" Smith asked, dazed. "What about America?"

"The United States possesses the largest expanse of fertile land in the world. For this reason, all of America will be converted to farmland. Your country will feed the world."

"We'll be farmers?"

"Indeed."

Smith sputtered. "Another 'final solution' by another lunatic," he shouted. "The world will laugh at you."

"Oh, but you're wrong. You underestimate the far-reaching effects of Phase One. The silent messages transmitted through television will continue to be broadcast until the world finds itself begging for its new leader. And Abraxas shall be there for them. On the twelfth of this month, I will reveal myself to all the people of the planet. The purpose of my broadcast will be to instruct them to follow me. They will listen, I assure you. They will follow me into the new age. And none will laugh."

The people at the table leaped to their feet, applauding and stamping. LePat took up the name of Abraxas in a chant, and the others joined him.

"I thank you," the deep voice said at last. "And now I wish for you all to see the work that the members of the Phase One task force have already begun. Circe, the lights, please."

The room dimmed.

"What you are about to see is recent film documenting actual occurrences around the world. It is the result of a program using the same type of subliminal television messages that worked so successfully with Mr. Peabody and the other assassins in our tests. The message that was broadcast in this case was the single word 'Abraxas.' If you will, Circe."

The projector clacked to life. Light flooded the blank screen. An image appeared of a throng of people gathered around the Eiffel Tower, their hands raised to the sky. The noise was deafening as the people in the film opened and closed their mouths in unison. "Abraxas!" they shouted again and again, the chant growing louder.

"Abraxas," called a crowd of thousands gathered near St. Stephen's Tower at the foot of Big Ben. "Abraxas," chanted a gathering of hundreds of saffron-robed Hindus before the reflecting pool of the Taj Mahal. Millions, from the factories of Peking to the streets of Nairobi, called the name of the new god. The chant was on the lips of Iowa farmers and Danish fishermen and Korean students and Russian sailors. "Abraxas," spoke the people of the world.

"My God," Smith said. Whatever madness had been committed, however the gears of Abraxas's terrible destructive machine had been put into motion, Smith knew only that he must reach the president.

But his attaché case was gone, and the portable telephone inside it. To warn the one man who could end Abraxas's reign of terror before it progressed further, Smith would have to escape the South Shore compound.

Overhead, the camera continued to swing in its arc above the darkened room. The delegates cheered as the film went on, chanting along with the masses on the screen.

He had a chance, Smith said to himself, eyeing the door. He hadn't seen any guards around the compound. It was dark in the room. If he could dash out of the place while the camera was angled away from him, he might be able to make a run for the village.

He waited for his moment. Then, when the group was roaring and the camera tilted toward the far left corner, he doubled over and ducked out of the room.

It was dark outside, the dirt road illuminated only by the moon and the stars. The fence surrounding South Shore was fairly tall, but Smith managed to climb it. At the top, he dropped over the side. A stabbing pain shot through his ankle.

He stood up and tested the leg. It was only a sprain, but the pain was bad. He told himself that he'd been hurt much worse during his years with the OSS and the CIA. That was a long time ago, but he hadn't forgotten his training. He scrambled quickly away from the fence and limped along the side of the road, traveling as fast as he could among the shadows.

The village was more than a mile away. By the time he reached the deserted main intersection, his ankle was throbbing with pain that pounded at him in waves. "The president," he mumbled. Once he found the telephone he was looking for, it didn't matter what Abraxas did to him. But he had to find that phone.

He had seen a telecommunications center on the outskirts of the village on his way into South Shore from the airport. From it, he had guessed that Abaco was one of those islands where private telephones were scarce, and most calls were made through one office. If his leg would only hold out until he reached the office, he could probably break into it.

Past the village, a small circle of light glowed on a winding side road. Smith recognized it. The telecommunications center was nearby. He forced his swelling ankle to move toward the light.

Below the bright circle the building stood, alone and vulnerable, its windows at eye level. Even with his useless leg, breaking into the place would be easy.

He picked up a rock and, spreading his coat over the window, broke it silently. Groaning from the pain in his leg, he managed to hoist himself up to the window and swing inside.

There was a switchboard, a primitive model Smith could figure out with one look. Crouched in the darkness, he whispered to the overseas operator and waited for the connection to click through to Washington.

"The White House. Good evening," the operator said after what felt like an interminable wait. Smith was sweating. His ankle pounded mercilessly.

"This is Dr. Harold W. Smith. I must speak with the president."

"I'm afraid that's not possible at this time, Mr. Smith," the operator said cheerfully. "Will you leave a message?"

"I assure you I'm not a crank," he said. "Please give the president my name. This is an urgent matter. And it's *Doctor* Smith."

"I've told you, Mr. Smith . . ."

He didn't hear the rest of her sentence. Outside, a car's headlights approached.

They followed me.

"I cannot reach the president through the channels I normally use," Smith persisted, glancing toward the headlights. They veered onto the side road, toward him. "This is a matter of top national security. Please tell him it's Harold Smith, and hurry. There isn't much time."

"Well, I don't know . . ."

"Tell him!" Smith hissed.

The car's engine droned louder as it neared

the building, then shut off suddenly. Two doors slammed. "Hurry!"

"All right," the operator said uncertainly. "But this better be for real."

"It is." He waited. Sweat poured down his face into the collar of his shirt. His heart felt like a frightened bird flapping inside his chest. The line was silent. "Please hurry," he whispered into the dead phone.

The doorknob turned and clicked as it hit the lock. Someone on the other side kicked at it. Smith watched the cheap wood bend with the blow.

The telephone crackled. "Hello? Hello?" Smith shouted. There was no response.

From behind the door came the explosion of a pistol fired at close range. The door shook on its hinges. A man's foot kicked it open. It was LePat, a Walther P-38 still smoking in his hand. Circe was with him. They walked toward him quickly, Circe fumbling with something in her handbag.

Smith followed them with his eyes, but he remained with the telephone. His life, he figured, was worth as little where he was as it would be five feet away. He wouldn't get much farther than that before LePat's Walther stopped him.

"Yes?" came the familiar voice on the other end of the line. Smith opened his mouth to speak, but only a gasp came out. He felt a sharp stab in the back of his neck. His veins turned to pasta. Out of the corner of his eye he saw Circe's long, manicured fingers depressing a plunger into a hypodermic filled with pink liquid.

"Mr. President," he drawled, sounding like a drunk. He said no more. His brain reeled with what felt like the blow of a cushioned hammer. He opened his lips to speak, but it was useless. As the room began to swirl and darken around him, he was aware only of the president's voice calling his name from a world away as LePat's hand hung up the receiver.

Chapter Eleven

Remo awoke with a start. He was fully dressed, lying on the floor of the hotel room. "What time is it?"

Chiun peered out the window. "Nearly nine."

"In the *morning*? You mean I've been asleep since yesterday afternoon?"

"You were tired," the old man said. "We both were. The journey was difficult."

"But I never sleep. Not like that, anyway." He got to his feet groggily. "The last thing I remember is watching television. . . ."

" 'Ways of Our Days,' " Chiun said, smiling. "You were entranced with it. A fine drama, don't you agree?"

"That's it," Remo said. "It was that idiotic soap opera. It gave me a headache. My brain felt like it was going to explode."

"Do not fear. It will never be full enough for that."

"You're a laugh a minute. Ouch." He pressed his fingers to his temples. Light flashed behind his closed eyelids. Lights, and a word printed in bold letters across a mesh of fine gray lines. "Chiun," he called, alarmed.

"What is it?"

"Abraxas. I see it. The word, I mean."

"You, too? Ah, well. The deity must have need of many disciples."

"Mrs. Peabody," Remo said in amazement.

"No, no. Mrs. Havenhold. The name of the heroine of 'Ways of Our Days' is Mrs. Havenhold."

"I mean Orville Peabody's wife. She saw the word, too. So did her son. Her son who *wasn't in school.* Get it? It was the television. 'Abraxas' was on the screen."

"I saw nothing on the screen."

"It had to be. Those gray lines you were talking about were the field behind the television picture. You can always see them if you look closely. See?" He turned on the television set. A children's program was on, showing a bunch of toddlers being led around a barnyard by a man in a rooster costume. Remo's head felt as if it were being constricted by steel wires. "It's still there," he said.

"Where?" The children squealed with delight as they picked up baskets of colorful plastic eggs from the henhouse.

"Somewhere. I can feel it."

"And I cannot?" Chiun asked archly. "Perhaps I am not sufficiently sensitive to receive this invisible message?"

"Perhaps you've spent a lot more time watching television than I have. A person's eyes have to get used to that flickering light. Mine have never adapted to it." He closed his eyes hard, then opened them. He repeated the motion.

"That is a ridiculous idea."

"Abraxas," Remo said slowly, blinking his eyes in a quick pattern. "There it is."

"Where?" Chiun demanded, staring at the screen, where nothing more pernicious than a bunch of children petting lambs was going on.

"Blink in rhythms of four, five, and nine," Remo said.

The old man blinked. "Abraxas," he whispered.

"In English, Korean, and every other alphabet in the world. We picked up the languages we were most familiar with, that's all. A little something for everybody."

"It was a trick," Chiun whispered, incredulous. "Abraxas is a fraud. A word on a television."

"Take it easy. It's not the end of the world."

"But *why*? Why would anyone do such a thing? Why would somebody want to ruin my beautiful drama?"

"I don't know." Remo ran a hand through his hair and bolted for the door. "But somehow I get the feeling that Smitty's disappearance is tied up in this, too."

He headed for South Shore. The gates were locked up but unguarded, and he vaulted easily over the top.

The compound was beautiful, with grounds covered by lush tropical gardens and dominated by a rambling old plantation house decorated with turrets and gingerbread trim. Just beyond the house lay a stretch of white-sanded beach that appeared to wind down the shoreline for several hundred yards. A few people strolled through the gardens, alone or in groups of two and three, but no one paid Remo any attention. They all seemed to be drinking, he noticed, remembering what the frightened black man on the road had told him about the activities at South Shore. What struck Remo as odd was that everyone was drinking the same pale pink beverage.

He caught a glimpse of white lace behind the aged folds of a eucalyptus tree. It was the woman with the scar. Her face was pensive and preoccupied as she stared into the distance. She didn't see Remo approach. Leaning against the tree, her hands folded behind her, she looked, Remo thought, like Alice in Wonderland.

"Am I interrupting anything?" Remo said.

She jumped. When she recognized Remo, her expression changed from surprise to fear.

"I don't give up easily," he said, smiling. "We had a date, remember?"

She cast a furtive glance over her shoulder. "You shouldn't be here," she whispered.

"Neither should Harold Smith."

To his surprise, she didn't deny any knowledge of Smith. Instead, she only stared into Remo's eyes. What he saw there puzzled him. She was Alice in Wonderland, all right, all white lace and sunshine, but it was a different Alice from the little girl of the storybooks, an older, sadder creature, irrevocably scarred by the past, looking with dread into the future.

"Look," Remo said. "What do you say we quit playing games and tell the truth."

She hesitated. "I wish I could," she said.

"I'll settle for Smith's whereabouts, for starters."

"Please leave."

"After you tell me."

She sighed. "All right. He's here. You knew that."

"Where here? It's a big place."

"It doesn't matter where. He won't leave with you now."

A chill ran down Remo's spine. "Is he dead?"

"No. Not dead. But he might as well be." She checked over her shoulder again. "Listen, I can't talk here."

"Hey, what kind of setup is this?"

"I'll explain it all to you later. Meet me at Mother Merle's tonight. It's a hangout for the locals on the north side of the island. Ten o'clock. I'll tell you everything then. But you must go now."

"I don't . . ."

"Please."

". . . Even know your name," Remo finished.

"My name isn't important," she said quietly. "They call me Circe. I'll be waiting for you." She fled from him like a frightened rabbit, the breeze blowing the white lace of her dress behind her as she vanished into the garden.

"Going somewhere, Circe?"

She gasped as LePat's hand snatched at her sleeve from behind an acacia tree. "Oh, it's you," she said, looking at the little man as if he carried disease.

"Who's the new beau?" LePat's voice was as oily as his plastered hair. "You know, Abraxas doesn't like us to fraternize with outsiders."

"He was . . . I just . . ."

"Let's tell Abraxas about this, shall we?" He took her arm and shoved her roughly ahead.

"Now, wait a minute," she said, shaking off his grip. "You've got no right to treat me like this. Abraxas will see to it that you're straightened out."

"Pretty sure of yourself, aren't you?" He smiled. Then, as suddenly as the smile had appeared, it was transformed into a menacing scowl. "Well, I'll let you in on something, missy. You may have been Abraxas's favorite once, but things have changed. This time you've gone too far. Last night was the beginning of the end for you."

"What about last night?" she demanded.

"You didn't like sticking that needle into Smith, did you?" he taunted.

"I did it, didn't I?"

"Abraxas doesn't think you're tough enough to stick with the program to the end."

"Don't be absurd. Where else am I going to go? It's just that I didn't think I'd have to harm anyone."

"That's just the attitude Abraxas doesn't like. That's why he's had me following you. Who's the trusted aide now?" he said with a smirk.

"You did what?"

"I followed you. And it's a good thing I did. You can't be trusted."

"I resent being trailed around like some kind of criminal," she said.

"Get inside." He nearly threw her through the screen doors of the mansion.

The two of them stood in front of the humming camera. "What is it?" Abraxas's voice rang out in the silence.

"I found her in the garden, sir," the little man said proudly. "She was talking with someone from outside. She probably let him through the gate herself."

"I did not," Circe objected.

"Who was this man?" the voice asked.

"I—I don't know his name. Just someone I met in town."

"What did he want?"

"He . . ." She stopped and looked up at the camera. "Why am I being interrogated like this?"

"You let Smith escape last night."

"But I went after him."

"You should have watched him more closely. It was your job."

"But it was dark. . . ."

"Who was the man you were talking to?"

"I tell you, I don't know his name!" she shouted. She closed her eyes and collected herself. "He was looking for Dr. Smith. He knows he's here."

"How does he know?" the voice demanded.

"He didn't tell me," Circe said defiantly. "I made

arrangements to meet him later. I thought you'd want to send someone to pick him up for questioning."

"Questioning?" The voice broke into a deep rumbling laugh. "An infiltrator comes into our midst—a spy—and you want me to *question* him?"

"Why, yes," Circe said, bewildered. "There may be others."

"He will be killed, as will any others that come after him."

"*Killed*? Without even giving him a chance to talk?"

"Death is the only way to deal with those outside our sphere of influence. Death is the only punishment that works."

"But what about everything you've said about unity?" she said, her voice small. "And harmony. And peace."

"Words are only words. The Great Plan will not be foiled by words. Death to traitors, Circe. Remember that."

"Traitors? Why are you talking to me like this? I'm not a traitor."

"No?" The question hung in the air. "Perhaps you were planning to lead the outsider into a trap, as you say. Perhaps. And perhaps you would have told me about it."

"I was going to, I swear it."

"She didn't head straight for the house after talking with him, sir," LePat said.

"I'm not a robot!" she screamed. "I wanted to think about it."

126

"Ah, yes. My Circe has become quite the thinker," Abraxas said. The voice darkened. "Thinking is my responsibility, not yours."

She quaked. "Yes, sir," she said.

"Were you . . . attracted to this man you met?"

"What kind of question is that?" she asked indignantly.

"Answer it! Were you attracted to him?"

She was silent for a long moment. "No," she said at last, her cheeks flaming.

"You're lying. And you're lying about not knowing his name."

"I *don't* know his name!"

"And you may be lying about your plans to turn him over to me. It would have been just as easy for you to turn me over to him."

"I would never do that to you, Abraxas. Never." Her voice was choking.

"Was he handsome?"

"No," she said, her cheeks burning.

"Lying again, my dear. Remember, I have known you for a long, long time. I have seen your eyes cloud with lust at the sight of a strong pair of arms and a handsome face."

"That's not fair," she said, weeping openly now. "I love you. I have never broken faith with you. I have never once lain with a man . . ."

"Enough," the voice on the loudspeaker commanded.

Circe glanced over to LePat, suddenly remembering his presence. "I have always been grateful to you," she said brokenly to Abraxas.

"I will let the episode pass with a warning. This time. But only this time. The next trespass will bring punishment, swift and sure and irrevokable. Do you understand?"

"I understand," Circe said, looking at the floor.

How had this happened? she asked herself. How far had the madness gone? Suddenly she saw herself as if she were another person looking into the room. There she stood, begging the forgiveness of a disembodied voice on a loudspeaker, trembling before the eye of a television camera, fearing for her life.

"What time is your meeting with this man?"

"Ten o'clock," she said numbly.

It wasn't going to be like this. It was never supposed to be like this.

"Where?"

The stranger. The stranger was her only hope. If she could only trust him with the truth. . . .

"I asked you where you were going to meet him."

She looked up with a start. "Where?" Her mind raced. Mother Merle's was on the north end of the island. "The Conch Inn," she lied. "Across from the fish market."

"That's near South Shore, isn't it?"

"Yes," she said, struggling to keep her eyes on the camera. If she were caught in this lie, she knew, there would be no second warning.

"You'll remain here. I'll send some hired men to go in your place and dispose of him. LePat, do you have a description of him?"

"I saw him myself, sir."

"Very well. You'll instruct the men. Circe, you may leave now."

She nodded obediently and walked out.

Tonight, she thought. Tonight her life was going to change forever, and whether she lived or died was going to depend on the whim of a total stranger whose name she didn't even know.

Chapter Twelve

"Remo. Remo."

Chiun had perfected a stage whisper that could reach across an ocean. Remo saw him now, a glimmer of blue satin resting motionless among the trees beyond the gate to South Shore. He trotted up the road and onto the hillside. "What is it?"

"There has been trouble. Someone stopped the woman you spoke with in the garden."

Remo shook his head. "She's a piece of work, that one," he said. "After she gives me the treatment with those big sad eyes of hers, she runs straight to her boss."

"It did not appear that way," Chiun said.

"It was, believe me. Anyone who calls herself Circe is bad news."

"A fitting name for a siren," Chiun said, smiling.

Remo shrugged. "Well, no big deal. Let her do what she wants. She might put us onto something. She says Smitty's in bad shape. You haven't seen him, have you?"

"No, but there are others. Behind the house, on the far shore."

Remo squinted into the distance. Along the beach milled a dozen or more people. The sea breeze carried their voices, merry and carefree. "Well, it's worth a look, I guess," Remo said. "But let's make it fast. From the way the girl talked, Smith's probably in a dungeon somewhere inside the house."

The shoreline was narrow and rocky, laced with the warm Caribbean waves that lapped up onto the blinding white sand. The revelers on the beach were a rowdy crowd, singing and joking, apparently comfortable with one another's company. There was little at the beach party to remind Remo of the strange goings-on that had led him here.

"Let's go," he said. "We're wasting our time. No one's holding Smith prisoner at this clambake."

"Are you sure?" the old Oriental asked. He raised his arm slowly to point at a figure seated near some craggy rocks a hundred feet away.

Remo walked closer. The figure was a middle-aged gray-haired man. He was dressed in fuscia-colored Bermuda shorts and a loose shirt printed with palm trees. A blue ribbon flapped on his collar. On his head was an electric-blue sun visor decorated with a portrait of Pierre LeToque, the underground symbol of marijuana. One hand held a champagne glass filled with frothy pink liquid; the other grasped a large sheet of green and white computer printout paper. Beside him a portable radio blasted reggae music at an ear-shattering level.

"Naah," Remo said. "It couldn't be him. You don't think it could be, do you?"

Chiun nodded serenely.

"Smitty?" he called, approaching the dapper figure.

"Ah lak a woman," the man sang, tapping his foot to the music.

"What the hell have they done to him?"

Smith downed the pink cocktail with a satisfying belch. He snatched a pencil from behind his ear and began scribbling furiously on the printout spread on his lap.

"Clearly the emperor has lost his mind," Chiun whispered.

"Clearly the emperor is shitfaced drunk," Remo said irritably, grabbing the glass out of Smith's hand. "What do you think you're doing?" he yelled. "We've been halfway around the world looking for you. You're supposed to be in some kind of terrible trouble. And here you are—"

"I've got it!" Smith exclaimed ecstatically. He seemed to notice the two figures at his side for the first time. "Why, Remo," he said, smiling so that all his teeth showed. "Hello, Chiun. What brings you here? Lovely weather." He went back to his scribbling.

"You bring us here," Remo said, wondering if he had ever before seen Smith smile. "You disappeared off the face of the earth a while back, remember?"

"I what? Well, I suppose so. It doesn't make

any difference, anyway. Would you two care for a cocktail?"

"No, thanks," Remo said.

"Good heavens, this is really it," Smith said softly, circling a section of the printout. "It stands up to all the proofs."

"All what proofs? What are you doing?"

"I've just found a way to program into the IRS computers," he said excitedly, vibrating the sheet on his lap. "It's unbelievably simple, really. All we have to do is transmit data from a remote computer as far away as half a mile from the main terminal, and then tap into the machines through ultra-short-wave codes in the underground telephone circuits. A child could have figured it out."

"I don't have any idea what you're talking about," Remo said.

"He meant a bright child," Chiun explained.

Smith tapped his pencil on his visor reflectively. "You know, we could do this in half the time using the Folcroft Four. Don't you agree?" He looked up at Remo eagerly. He giggled. "So long, IRS. So long, U.S. budget. Hello, sunshine."

"What? Use the Folcroft computers to rip off the IRS? Have you lost your mind?"

"I told you that in the beginning," Chiun said in Korean.

"*Au contraire,*" Smith said debonairly. "I've *found* my mind. At long last, I've discovered the reason for being. This is all for the good of mankind, don't you see?" He waved the printout gaily. "We mustn't stand in the way of mankind, after all. Abraxas wouldn't like it."

"*Abraxas*? You, too?"

"I wonder if the British tax banks are as easy to crack as ours. Hmmm." He absorbed himself in drawing a series of intersecting lines on the printout.

"We've got to get him out of here."

"The boat is that way," Chiun said, gesturing toward the left. "I suggest we take the sea route."

"I suppose so," Remo said, lifting Smith. "They won't look for him in the water. . . ."

"Let me down!" Smith shouted. "What's the idea of breaking in here where you haven't been invited, and then . . . Help! Help!"

Chiun raised an eyebrow. "Sorry, Smitty," Remo said as he pressed two fingers into the back of Smith's neck. The gray-haired man slumped silently into Remo's arms.

"What do you think got into him?" Remo asked as he laid the inert figure of Smith on a bunk in one of the yacht's luxurious cabins. "Did you catch the business about Abraxas?"

"A vile trick. I shall destroy the shrine. Worse, I will give it back to the library."

"I'll settle for destroying the people who did this to Smitty," Remo said.

"Well . . ."

"Well, what?"

"Don't act too hastily. He *was* rather pleasant," Chiun said wistfully.

"Oh, never mind. You stay with him. I'm going back to South Shore."

"But why? We have the emperor."

"We have Smith's body," Remo said, indicating the unconscious man on the bunk. "The girl told me he might as well be dead. We don't know what's going to happen to him. Or to any of us, for that matter. That Abraxas stuff on the television has me spooked."

"It's very strange," Chiun said. "If I saw it in New York City, and you saw it here, and someone in Ohio saw it also . . ."

"Right. A lot of people are seeing it. Including Smith, who suddenly decided to pirate the IRS computer banks. God only knows what else is going on inside that mansion on the beach."

"I agree," Chiun said. "I will stay here with the emperor. What will you do?"

"I've got a date," Remo said.

Mother Merle's was packed to bursting with islanders, their faces glistening with sweat as they danced to the lazy, hypnotic steel drum music of the band. In the corner, her face lit by the flickering light of a candle, sat Circe, the only white face in the crowd. She was smoking. The glowing red tip of her cigarette trembled in the darkness.

"Alone?" Remo said. "I'm surprised. When's the ambush?"

She took his hand. Her face, he saw, was lined with worry. "You've got to help me," she whispered.

"Oh, I think you've got enough help."

"I don't understand—"

"Come on. You're part of that group of kidnap-

136

pers on the beach. Even the islanders know about you. And someone saw you running to your boss as soon as you left me back there in the garden. So suppose you cut the crap and try to do what you're going to do with me."

She stared at him with big, luminous eyes that welled with tears. "Abraxas is planning to kill you," she said. "He can do it. He's killed before."

"Peabody?"

"He arranged that. Others, too."

"I wish someone would tell me who this Abraxas is. It would make things a lot easier."

"He's my employer."

Remo smiled. "That little squirt?"

"No. That's LePat. Abraxas sent him to spy on me. He caught me talking to you. I told him I had set a trap for you so that his men could kill you."

"Did you?"

She lit another cigarette from the one still burning and inhaled deeply. "Yes," she said.

"True to form."

"But I didn't go through with it," she said quickly. "I gave him the name of another place on the other side of the island. His men are checking there now. They'll come here eventually. I thought you'd help me get away from him, but . . ." She buried her face in her hands.

"Hey, c'mon," Remo said, placing his hand over hers. "It can't be that bad."

"How could you ever trust me, after the way I've treated you?"

"Who said I trusted you?" Remo said. "What happens if whoever's gunning for me finds you?"

"I'll be killed. Whether they find you or not, Abraxas will destroy me now. I've lied to him."

"This Abraxas sounds like one terrific guy."

"He's insane," she said quietly. "I realized that today." A sob started deep in her chest and bubbled out of her. "How could things have gone this far?" she shrilled. "I never thought—I'm afraid. I'm so afraid."

"Let's get out of here," Remo said, pulling her to her feet. "We'll go someplace where you can tell me about this setup from the beginning."

"All right," Circe said, picking up her handbag with shaking hands. "There's a place along the shoreline . . ." She gasped. The pocketbook fell to the floor.

"What is it?" He followed her eyes to the doorway, where eight big black men stood. They held clubs, and their steely eyes were riveted on Remo and the girl. As Remo watched, the men walked toward them slowly. "We've got company," Remo said. "Did you bring your car?"

She nodded, the corners of her mouth white with saliva.

"Get in it and wait for me."

"But there are too many of them—"

"Go. Run." He pushed her out of the way of the oncoming thugs.

Two of the men swung sticks above their heads. The music faded to scattered, tuneless sounds, then died. A woman's scream set off the stampede for the door. People rushed everywhere,

138

overturning tables and knocking each other down as they hurried to clear the room for the lone white man surrounded by a circle of paid fighters.

One of the thugs hurled his club at Remo's head. Remo held out his arm, palm flat, and met the blow squarely. The club shattered in the man's hand. Then, with one finger, Remo lodged the man's nose up into his brain while he kicked out at the tightening circle. Two more fell, groaning, to the floor.

The air whistled. So swift that it was almost invisible, a leather cat-o'-nine-tails cracked, its metal-tipped streamers shooting out toward Remo's chest.

"In the holy name of Abraxas," the man holding the whip cried.

"In the holy name of Holy Mackerel," Remo said. With a subtle motion of his hands, he extended his fingertips to meet the steel ends of the cat. The tiny balls sprang back with nine chiming pings and embedded themselves like bullets into the forehead of the man who held the whip. He stood stock still for a moment, the nine red holes in his head too deep to bleed, as his eyes glazed and he fell forward over a table with a crash.

They were all on him now, fists pummeling the air as again and again they pounded at the thin young man with the thick wrists who moved so quickly that no one could strike him. A head splintered against a wall, gushing blood like a fountain; one man armed with a long knife wailed in terror as he beheld his weapon in his right

hand and the bloody stump where his left had
been. The smell of death crept into the dim,
sweat-smelling room as men screamed and
prayed against the magic of the white man who
could kill as easily as he breathed.

Then the lights went out. The already shadowy
room was plunged into utter darkness.

Remo widened his pupils to see. A few men
were left, strewn around the floor waiting in despair for their final death blows. No one was
fighting anymore.

"Tell Abraxas he's next," Remo said, and walked
out.

The white Opel was waiting by the doorway.
As Remo climbed in, it skidded away down the
dirt road.

"Was it you who pulled the lights?" he asked.

Circe nodded. "I thought it would help you
escape. The odds were somewhat against you."
She stuck a cigarette into her mouth and lit it with
violently trembling fingers.

"You smoke too much," Remo said. "Keep
that up, and you won't live long."

She expelled a dry, bitter little laugh and drove
on.

Chapter Thirteen

She turned off into a wooded copse where the scrub pines concealed the car from the road. It was a dark night, overcast by heavy clouds that hid the moon from view.

"The shore's down there, past the hill," Circe said, gesturing forward with her chin. "You can't see it tonight, but there's a cave nearby. We can talk there."

"Don't you think you're being a little paranoid?" Remo said, picking his way through the sharp rocks along the deserted beach. Big tufts of algae and sea grass grew in the sand holes where the water gushed in rhythmically and, hissing, withdrew. "No one could have followed us here."

"You don't know Abraxas," she said. The red glow of her cigarette led him into a cool place smelling of sea and everlasting darkness.

"The cave I spoke about," Circe said. "We'll be safe here." She settled into a moss-covered cleft of smooth rock. "I don't even know where to begin."

"Start with Abraxas. Who is he?"

His eyes were already at home in the darkness. Circe sat on her haunches, her arms wrapped around her knees, as she began to pick up the threads of the story that had ended here for her, in this secret place, begging a stranger for help.

"Abraxas isn't his read name," she said hesitantly. "His real name is Perseus Mephisto. His father was a shipping tycoon."

"Greek?"

"Yes. I, too, am Greek, although I've spent much of my life traveling." She lit a cigarette off the butt still glowing between her fingers. "The Mephisto family was very wealthy. In their house at Corinth alone, more than fifty servants were housed. I was one of them."

Remo said, "You don't act like anybody's servant."

"I'm not anymore. Not exactly, anyway." She sighed. "I was young when I lived in Corinth. Both my parents worked for the family, and I did small chores around the house to help my mother. Perseus was already a young man by the time I was ten years old. He used to tell me that when I grew up I would be beautiful." Involuntarily, she touched the scar on her face.

"He was right about that," Remo said, removing her hand. "You are."

She took a deep drag from her cigarette. "I adored him. All I remember about my youth is Perseus. Perseus, on his father's great ship, the wind ruffling his hair. Perseus coming home on his visits from the university, running up the servants' staircase to lift me so high, I could touch the ceiling. Perseus . . . it was always Perseus. He was as brilliant and warm as the sun itself, and handsome as a god."

"Are we talking about the same man?" Remo asked. "The one who's trying to kill us both?"

"He's different now," she said softly. Her eyes were strange and faraway, as if trying to envision a past as distant and removed from the present as a drugged dream.

"It didn't happen all at once. I started to notice the change in him when Perseus entered the family business. He was the firstborn son. In a family like the Mephistos, that's like being heir to a throne. Perseus was groomed to take over his father's empire."

"What happened? Didn't he measure up to his old man? Happens all the time," Remo said, thinking briefly of Chiun.

"Quite the opposite," Circe said. "From what I understood, he was brilliant. His mother was very proud of him. But after seeing his son's successes, his father complained that Perseus was too rash and too independent. I think that Mephisto was envious of his son's ability. He was an arrogant man, and hated it when Perseus went against him on matters of policy, even though his son's ideas were usually better than his own." She paused as if collecting her thoughts.

"It was around that time that Perseus began to confide in me. I was still young, but I was no longer a child. He often told me that I was wise

143

beyond my years, and that was why he trusted me. Actually, though, I think I was his only friend during those months. I was fifteen."

"Was he your lover?"

"No. He was not like ordinary men, even then. He shunned women—all personal contacts, really. He said that great men must stand alone." She smiled. "He called me his siren," she said. "I was the temptation that whetted his appetites and gave him strength. In some twisted way, he believed that by resisting me he became greater."

"I remember that story from school," Remo said. "Listening to the sirens' song without giving in to it. What is it? Ulysses?"

"Exactly. That's when he began to call me Circe. To tell the truth, I like thinking of myself that way. It was a far cry from the cleaning girl I was during the days. It made me love him more than ever.

"Then one day he told his father of his plans to take over the business. Mephisto laughed at him. He said he wouldn't be ready to retire for years. He hurt Perseus even more by saying he was going to bring his younger sons into the business as well. For Perseus, it was an insult beyond bearing. He came to me that evening, still trembling with anger. He called his father terrible things, and said that the old man's time had passed. He said he would take power from his father. 'How?' I asked him. He said, 'I'll have to kill him.'

"It made me shiver. He was so calm. If I hadn't loved him so much, I would have run to tell the old man. But Perseus was my god, and if he'd asked me to kill Mephisto myself, I would have done it for him."

"How was he going to do it?"

"Fire. It was Mephisto's habit to visit the warehouses on Saturdays, including an old building used to store lumber on the outskirts of the city. Perseus waited until his father and all the workers were inside, then poured kerosene around the building and set a match to it. The place burned to the ground, but Perseus's father escaped without any injuries.

"His father never mentioned the incident. Perseus was worried that Mephisto knew who had started the fire and would try to get even with him, but as the weeks passed, he came to believe that Mephisto viewed the fire as an accident. Then one day Perseus told me that Mephisto had asked him to take the family's big yacht, the *Pegasus*, to Sardinia to pick up some relatives who were vacationing there. I sneaked out of the house when the ship was ready to sail so that I could watch it leave harbor. Perseus waved to me from the deck. . . ."

She brushed a tear from her face. "When the ship was about a mile out of the harbor, the sky lit up in a blaze, and I heard a sound, a terrible sound like the gates of hell crashing shut. Fragments of metal and wood shot up from the ship, and columns of black smoke poured out of it. The smoke looked like blood in water, dark and spreading, filled with death.

"I didn't take time to think. All I knew was that the man I loved was on that ship, and I had to get to him somehow. I cut loose a small boat with an outboard motor and headed out toward the *Pegasus.* Even from a half-mile away, the air was hot and choking from the smoke. I could barely see. Then, when I was more than halfway to the ship, a second explosion turned the *Pegasus* into a ball of fire. Debris was flying everywhere.

"I stood up in the boat to try to get my bearings, since I couldn't see through the smoke. I didn't see the thing coming at me. A splinter from the deck, maybe, or part of the steel plating—I never found out. Whatever it was, it hit me in the face like a hot knife, so hard that it knocked me overboard. Now that I think back on it, it must only have been a glancing blow, or else I would have lost consciousness. I managed to find the boat somehow and crawl back into it. Something flooded into my eyes. I brushed them, and my hands came away covered with blood, my blood. It was everywhere—pouring down my clothes, falling in big drops onto the planks of the boat. I never saw so much blood. I thought I was dying. All I wanted to do at that point was to reach Perseus before it happened. For some reason, I never doubted that he was alive. Perseus was too big for death. But when I saw him, I remember wishing for a moment that he had died." Circe dabbed at her eyes with the back of a hand.

"I found him clinging to a wooden rafter in the water. His face was unrecognizable, a mass of burned flesh and teeth. All the skin had been burned off. I knew him only from his rings, which were melted into his fingers. One of his eyes was dangling from its socket. The bones of both legs had been shattered. His back was broken."

Circe's voice quavered with the memory. She placed one hand over her eyes and breathed shallowly, trying to pull back the tears.

"I don't know how I got him in the boat. The next thing I remember is the hospital. I was given blood and released after a few days. Perseus didn't leave for two years."

She lit a cigarette. "His mother died of heart failure then. Perseus was still far from recovered, but she had been paying for the operations he needed out of her own fortune. After she died, his father refused to pay the medical bills, and Perseus was moved to a clinic for the poor.

"I worked at what odd jobs I could. The wound on my face healed badly. This is the scar from it," she said bitterly, brushing her hand along her cheek. "Still, I was the lucky one. Perseus never completely healed."

"How is that?"

"In many ways. His body, of course, was permanently damaged, but his mind was broken, too. He knew his father had tried to kill him. I rented a small room for myself in the slum district of Corinth, and Perseus came to stay with me after his release from the clinic. He talked of nothing except his hatred for his father. Killing him wasn't good enough, he said. He wanted to hurt Mephisto in such a way that death would be welcome. He lived on hate in those days, and I encouraged him, because he had nothing else.

"To pass the days, he read—philosophy, theology. Ideas, I thought, to help him accept his condition. He took the name of Abraxas for himself. It was what the all-god of the ancients was called. 'Abraxas was once the most powerful force on earth,' Perseus told me. 'I plan to resurrect him.'

"As soon as he was able, he began to write letters—hundreds of them, it seemed—to his father's enemies asking them for money. Before the year was out, replies started to come in. Men from all over the world who wanted to see Mephisto's empire crumble lent him money to begin a business in direct competition with his father's. They didn't know how badly he'd been hurt, of course. He organized a small group of shipping experts, mostly men who'd once worked for Mephisto. The company was a success. Inside of three years, his investors had all been repaid and Mephisto, growing older and disappointed in Perseus's younger brothers, watched the business he had spent his life building begin to falter.

"Abraxas did a funny thing then. He got me a tutor. He said that an education could give me more than any man could offer." She stared into the blackness of the cave, her eyes pinched. "Now that I think of it, I was going to leave him then. I'd done what I could, and didn't want to spend the rest of my life as his nurse; he could afford all the help he needed by then, anyway. But he must have known that I wouldn't turn down a gift like that. Everyone has his price, I suppose," she said softly.

"At any rate, after I'd learned enough to go to a university, he sent me to the Sorbonne in Paris to study. After that, he sent me on a tour of the world. Once in a while I would read in the newspapers about Abraxas's businesses. He had branched out into many different areas, taking care to keep each business small so as not to attract too much attention. The shipping company itself was a fraction of the size of his father's, but along with it were companies that controlled the piers of major sea trading cities, trucking firms, warehouses, graneries, dairies, importing firms— everything that affected shipping. Together Abraxas's companies squeezed Mephisto's into bankruptcy. Abraxas himself bought the house his father had built. Before the old man was off the grounds, a demolition crew was sent in to level the building to the ground.

"Three months later Mephisto shot himself. Abraxas sold his businesses and called me home.

"That was five years ago. We came to live here in Abaco. He said he needed to be in a remote place. I thought he chose the island because of his health—that this would be a kind of quiet retirement for him. But as soon as we arrived at South Shore, he began work on what he calls his Great Plan. In it, he has set himself up as a god, using the entire population of the earth as pawns in a foolish game. That's what I thought it was, a game. I didn't see any harm in all his crazy talk at first. It was just the rambling of a bitter, crippled man removed from the rest of the world. But others took him seriously. LePat—his lackey—is paid an enormous salary to cater to Abraxas's whims. His latest whim was to assemble a hundred of the best minds in the world to help him carry out his plan."

She paused. "They're doing it, you know. Do you understand? This time he's destroying the whole world. And he won't stop until he obliterates it just as he did his father."

Her voice had gone hoarse. A pile of cigarette butts littered the floor at her feet. She looked small, her arms wrapped closely around her body, the long mark on her face illuminated by the eerie phosphorescence of fireflies. She looked over at him. "Well, that's all of it." She smiled ruefully. "I don't even know your name."

"Remo," he said, moving close to her. "I don't know yours, either."

"My parents disowned me long ago for saving Abraxas. Circe is all I have now. I'm used to it."

"Then come to me, Circe." He kissed her. She trembled in his arms. "Don't be afraid."

"It's not him I'm afraid of," she said softly. "I've never been with a man before."

Remo smiled, surprised. "What? The sophisticated lady of the islands, a virgin?"

"I've always felt as if I belonged to Abraxas. He held me with awe and pity and fear. But I don't want to belong to him anymore." She touched his face. "Remo, will you love me?"

"Loving you is easy," Remo said. He brushed her cheek with his lips. She found his mouth, and her tongue searched out his own. Then he undressed her gently, and on the cool, secret earth of the cave, serenaded by the rushing sea, he awakened her body with his. Later, they lay side by side.

"What's that?" Remo said, sitting up. He cocked his head toward the mouth of the cave.

Circe snatched up her clothes. "What's what?"

"I thought I heard something." He got dressed quickly. "Let's go. Something's changed."

"What?" she asked, shaken.

"It's nothing for you to worry about. Just the air. There's a presence here."

"How can you tell?"

"It would be too hard to explain," Remo said. He took her outside and led her by the hand back to the car. "Wait here." He closed the door after her.

"What did you hear?" she insisted.

"Maybe nothing. A hum, I thought. Something electric." He left her and walked silently into the brush.

"A hum?" Circe whispered. "Here?" Her face went ashen. She fumbled with the door handle. "No," she screamed, tripping out of the car. "Don't go in there! Remo!"

Another noise came then, clear and distinct: the crack and whine of a bullet in the instant before it struck the girl. She cried once, softly, before she fell.

Chapter Fourteen

Remo bent low over the girl to hear her words. "The car." She coughed, grimacing at the pain.

The bullet had hit her in the chest, although it struck well away from the heart. On the bright white of her dress grew a spreading bloom of red. "I should have known Abraxas would have the car tracked."

"Don't talk," he said. "You'll be all right. Just let me get you to a doctor."

"Help me . . ."

He felt the second bullet as soon as it was out of the pistol. It came toward him, parting the air in front of it in a miniature shock wave that stormed Remo's acute senses like the crude blow of a hammer. He threw himself over the girl. An instant later the bullet whizzed over his head, followed by the sharp crack of the report in the shadows of the scrub pines.

He was up before its echo died, moving swiftly through the darkness. Not a twig cracked beneath his feet. The silence that the bullet had broken was restored, and the air was still as he moved with the almost instinctive care of those trained in the arts of Sinanju.

He stopped. There was no sound. Chiun could walk with no sound, but few others could. Remo doubted that anyone who needed to use a gun to kill possessed the skill to run without disturbing the earth beneath his feet. He looked up. The man who'd shot Circe had to be waiting for him nearby. Ahead of him there was nothing. Behind, only the cheerful racket of mating sparrows.

"This way," a voice called from Remo's left. It was amused, mocking. Remo dashed for it, plunging through the trees and into a swamp of mangroves rising out of the mist like the spears of warriors.

"A little further." The voice sounded nearer. Whoever it was hadn't moved.

The swamp grew denser. The water reached up to Remo's knees. Above him, a low wind sighed through the spindly trees like a prayer for the dead, and the motionless fog hung like a pall around him. He felt as if he had stepped into another world, a primeval place half land and half water, stirring silently in darkness.

He moved with difficulty. The mud at the bottom of the swamp was getting thicker with each step he took. He felt as if he were walking on oatmeal. He grabbed hold of one of the upright mangroves. It bent in his hands like wet straw. Around him, as far as he could see, was nothing but swampland, swarming with the rush of mosquitos and sand flies.

The water was nearly to his waist now. His feet barely moved in the slimy bog at the bottom. He looked around. Which way had he come? And how far? It all looked the same. Everywhere was the thick soup of the fog and the ropy mangroves, stationed like sentinels in a lost prison stinking of decay.

"You're almost there ... Remo," the voice called.

"Who are you? How do you know my name?"

A little man with slicked hair and a Walther P-38 in his hand appeared seemingly out of nowhere. "I was listening," he said.

Remo lunged at him. It took all his strength to wade even inches through the mire. Perspiration popped up on his forehead as he struggled to lift one foot and then the other.

"I'm waiting," the man said.

Remo felt as if he were in a dream. The muck seemed to pull at him like a living thing. He stretched out his arms in front of him. Anything, a stick, a rock, he thought, anything to pull him out of this pit. But even the mangroves had disappeared from the bubbling black slime that clung to him.

"Quicksand," the man said amiably. "Amazing stuff, isn't it?" He walked forward, examining his pistol. He was right in front of Remo, standing at the edge of the bog. With two more steps, Remo could take hold of the man and kill him.

If he could take two steps.

"Oh. Allow me to introduce myself. Michael LePat. I work for Abraxas. Incidentally, that was his

155

woman you just raped. What a pity we won't get to know each other better." He smiled.

Remo was sinking faster. The quicksand tightened around his chest, easing the air out of his lungs slowly. He knew that if he panicked, the pit would swallow him whole. He held completely still and cleared his mind. Chiun had told him that, in situations where no answer was at hand, the voice of the gods spoke through a man's quiet mind. So he forced himself to be still, inside and out, while the hungry sea of quicksand churned around him.

No gods' voices came. Only a story Chiun had once told him about one of his ancestors who had ruled the ancient House of Sinanju. This Master of Sinanju, spoke Chiun, had passed his 120th year, and his strength was fading. In his dotage, while the Master lay in a bed of raw silk and gold waiting to pass quietly into the great void of death, a group of ruffians, to avenge a relative whom the Master had vanquished in his youth, stole him away to an unworthy place so that the old man would die in dishonor. They forced him to journey night and day to their own country to a cold crag overlooking a wasteland of rock.

"You will jump from this place to be smashed upon the rocks below," one of the abductors told the Master of Sinanju. "Your death will be one of weakness, a suicide, and the pain will be great."

The Master viewed the crag with his old eyes, which had seen the wonders of the world, and said, "I will do as you wish. I will jump from the crag and fall as the gods see fit. I ask only that you grant me one request before I pass into the void."

"We will do nothing to delay the wretched death you deserve," one of the murderers said.

"It will delay nothing. I ask only that you all stand near me to witness my end. As you can see, I am an old man, and no longer possess the power to fight you. All I wish for are witnesses to my death, so that those of my village will know truly that their Master has been defeated by a force greater than his own."

The ruffians swelled with pride. To tell the people of Sinanju that they had watched the Master die in ignominy and disgrace would satisfy their thirst for revenge.

"Very well, old man," their leader said, and the criminals advanced upon the crag to join the Master.

They did not see, as their aged prisoner had seen, that the crag was brittle and cracked and could not support the weight of many men. The crag broke free with a deafening splinter of rock and falling earth, dashing the men against the stones below. But the Master himself was prepared, and leaped away before the crag broke.

He returned in time to his village, and lived for thirty more years. Until his death, which was as quiet and dignified a passage into the void as any man could wish for, the Master was known throughout the Orient as the wisest of men.

Remo didn't know why the story had come into his head, but it gave him an idea. It offered a slim chance for escape, but more than he'd had a few moments before.

"Throw me a rock," Remo panted.

"A rock?" LePat raised his eyebrows in merriment. "You mean a rope, don't you? Sorry, I'm all out of rescue equipment."

"A rock," Remo insisted. "I'll sink faster."

LePat's expression was puzzled. "You talk as if you want to die."

"If it's going to happen, I'd like to get it over with. Come on, you've won. I know you'd rather see me go this way than with a bullet."

"Don't try to goad me," the little man said. "A bullet's too painless. You won't get me to shoot you."

"You don't have to shoot me. I'm willing to die in this crud. Just throw me a rock to get things moving, okay?"

LePat looked at him for a moment, appraising, then shrugged. "Why not," he said, hefting a slime-covered stone the size of a canteloupe. "Watching you die is becoming a bore, anyway." He tossed it carelessly to Remo.

With the palm of his hand Remo slapped back hard at the stone, putting a lot of English on it with his fingertips. It careened around in an arc, flying in a curve past LePat.

The little man ducked and stared at the flying rock as it whizzed by in its wide circle. "I should have known you'd try a trick," he said, aiming the Walther at Remo. He squinted, his lips curling into a sneer. "I think I'll only wound you. The shoulder, perhaps?" He veered the sight slightly to the right. "Don't hope to die from this bullet, by the way. I'm a considerably better shot than you are. That rock was the wildest toss I ever saw."

Remo said nothing. He was listening to the pitch of the air as the rock reached the farthest point in its curve and came back around, singing.

"Are you afraid, Remo?" LePat taunted.

"Simply quaking."

His throw had been good. The rock was right on target. At the moment when LePat's finger tensed to squeeze the trigger, the rock slammed him in the middle of his back, sending the gun splattering into the quicksand with the falling form of LePat behind it. As LePat stretched out his arms to reach for the gun, Remo lurched forward and grasped both the man's hands.

LePat cried out, his legs scrambling for purchase on the solid ground beyond the quicksand. Remo counted on the man's fear. The harder LePat struggled, the closer he brought Remo to the edge of the quagmire.

It was receding. The iron grip across his chest eased, and Remo could breathe again. The extra oxygen pumped into his arms in a surge of energy. With a monumental effort he pushed himself ahead and clasped his hands behind LePat's back. The little man cursed as he pulled back, saving himself from the quicksand and dragging Remo up with him.

"Thanks a million, pal," Remo said. He set one foot on the bank. Then, going into a deep spin, he swung the man into the air and released him.

LePat screamed as he landed chest first in the

quicksand. His arms flailed briefly, like the wings of a trapped insect, and then his breath released in a boil of filthy bubbles. His head disappeared first. The rest of him followed quickly. When Remo left him, all that remained above ground were LePat's shoes, which had come loose and floated upside down on the bog like the footprints of the doomed.

"Circe!" Remo called, running back through the scrub pines. He had found his way to the shoreline, and followed it back to the cave. Now, as he retraced his steps, he spotted the white car.

The place beside it where the girl had lain was empty.

The car. He went back to it and made a quick examination. Just as Circe had said, there was a small transmitter taped to the Opel's underside. With the strength of rage, he hurled the tracker high into the air and into the sea beyond. Then he returned to the place where he'd left the girl.

The ground was cold. She'd been moved some time ago. It could have been the police, he thought. But there were no tire tracks besides the Opel's. There was only one other explanation.

LePat hadn't been alone.

Remo got on his hands and knees in the grass by the car. He widened his pupils to maximum. The action made the blades of grass glimmer with unseen light. And on the grass were spots. They looked like water, but these spots were dark and thick and already beginning to harden. He rubbed some on his fingers and sniffed.

Blood.

She had left a trail for him.

The moon came out for a moment, illuminating the bloodstains to the road, where they continued. Toward South Shore. Whoever took Circe hadn't used a car.

A cloud passed overhead, blotting out the brief light of the moon, and a wave of sorrow passed over Remo. He was not a seer, but he knew when death was near. It was brushing against him now, and he knew that before the night was over, death would fold its dark wings and claim its victory.

Chapter Fifteen

A shiver of apprehension ran down Chiun's spine. Ever since he heard the shots fired from the island, he, too, felt the wings of death flapping in the night breeze. Remo could take care of himself against bullets. But there was something else on *that island, something indefinable and dangerous. It was as if the black cloud that obscured the stars was covering the whole earth, with the spectre of death heralding a new Dark Age.

Smith lay on the bunk where Remo had placed him. His eyelids fluttered. He looked at Chiun groggily.

"Where are we?" he whispered.

"Ah, Emperor Smith. You have come back to us at last. We are on a boat. It is safe here. Remo is on the island."

Smith shook himself awake. "My head," he said, cradling his head in his hands. "It feels like . . ."

"Like you drank too much?" Chiun offered.

"I beg your pardon? I don't drink."

"You did. Quite a bit, in fact, o illustrious one. You were, as Remo would say, doused."

"Soused," Smith corrected, groaning. "It's coming back to me now. The injection . . . those pink cocktails. Good God. The printouts."

"They are here. We brought you from that place."

"Thank you," he said, raising himself to his feet. Chiun handed him his clothes. "I can't imagine what would have happened if Abraxas got hold of them."

"You have seen him?"

"No. No one's seen him; just his name. It's been transmitted by satellite into every television set in the world. People are beginning to think that Abraxas is some kind of god."

"The masses are fools, easily duped," Chiun said loftily, averting his eyes. "But surely no one is in danger because of a name on a television set."

"That's just the beginning," Smith said, climbing into his trousers. "He's got a plan—the Great Plan, he calls it, the arrogant swine—to take over the world."

Chiun laughed aloud. "Others have tried that, most worthy emperor."

"He can do it," Smith said earnestly. "I know it's preposterous, but he's got everything organized to the last detail. You'll forgive me if I don't tell you the exact nature of his ideas. It's a matter of national security."

"Of course," Chiun said, trying to sound as if

he cared one way or the other about national security.

Smith buttoned his shirt hastily. "What we've got to concern ourselves with now is stopping him before this insanity goes any further. Can we reach Remo?"

"I am not his nursemaid," Chiun sniffed. "But he will show up. Bad pennies always do."

"Very well," Smith muttered. "Then we'll have to do this without him. I'll tell you some of what I know, but I must have your oath never to reveal what I am about to say."

"The Master of Sinanju gives his word," Chiun said, stifling a yawn.

Smith breathed deeply. When he spoke, his voice was weighted with urgency. "Abraxas is planning to reveal himself on worldwide television. He's going to interrupt broadcasts all over the world to announce the Great Plan of Abraxas. If that happens, the people he's hypnotized will support the massive destruction he's going to suggest. It will be too late to stop him then."

Chiun thought. "But how can everyone see him at once? Half the world sleeps while the other half lives in daylight."

"He's projected a time when all the communications satellites orbiting above earth will be in optimum position to broadcast to their widest possible range." He toyed sheepishly with his shirt button. "I did it for him, actually, from the compound's computer center. I—er—wasn't quite myself."

"Perfectly understandable, o worthy emperor," Chiun said. "You were doused."

"Messages have been transmitted from individual satellites telling people when to tune in. He's expecting an audience of a half-billion."

"Interesting."

"A half-billion people is enough to begin a world revolution."

"I see. And when will this announcement occur?"

"On the twelfth. One minute after midnight on the twelfth. That's odd. On the island I seem to have lost all track of time. What date is it today?"

"The eleventh," Chiun said.

"The *eleventh*?" Smith checked his watch. The color drained from his face. "It's eleven-twenty," he said.

On the South Shore grounds, Chiun regarded the rambling old manor house. "A strange place," he said.

"I suppose so," Smith panted, already exhausted from rowing the rubber raft that brought them from the yacht. Scaling the high fence onto the grounds had not been easy, either. Smith marveled at the uncanny strength of the old Oriental, who must have passed his eightieth year. For him the fence had been a child's barricade, crossed without effort. But then Chiun, he remembered, was special, just as Remo was special. Among the three, Smith alone was vulnerable to fatigue and weakness.

He wanted to rest. His head was still swimming from the effects of the drinks. He would never be young again, and, unlike Chiun, age and mortality weighed heavily on him. "Let's go in," he said.

"Are there no guards?"

"Unnecessary. Everyone here is fanatically devoted to Abraxas, and outsiders don't come in. They claim the place holds evil spirits, or some such nonsense."

"It may not be nonsense," Chiun said quietly. "I do not like the feel of this house."

The interior of the mansion was a labyrinth of small rooms connected by obscure passageways. In the distance were the muffled sounds of voices.

"They all must be in the conference room," Smith said. He glanced at his watch again. "Waiting for the broadcast."

"We do not have enough time to search all the rooms," Chiun said.

"I don't think we have to. If I can get into the computer center, I might be able to stop him from there."

"A machine cannot stop a maniac," Chiun scoffed.

"I'm going to try to get the codes for transmission and scramble them," Smith whispered as they headed down a series of empty, twisting corridors. "You see, the transmissions are beamed off satellites using codes translated into microwave emissions. . . ." He looked at Chiun, whose eyes were rolling. "Never mind," he said. "Follow me."

"As you wish."

The door to the computer room was locked. "Is this a problem?" Smith asked.

Chiun poked it with a fast jab of his index finger. The steel plate surrounding the knob shattered and fell to the floor like shards of glass. "No," Chiun answered.

There were only four items in the room: the computer console, a utilitarian chair placed behind it, a television monitor suspended from the ceiling, and the omnipresent camera. Smith sucked in his breath sharply at the sight of the camera. It was stationary. No hum issued from it. He waved his hand in front of it.

"It's not operating," he said finally. "Watch the door."

He sat down at the console. Then, his hands moving like a concert pianist's, he prepared the computer for conversation.

"GIVE PRESENT LOCATIONS OF COMMUNICATIONS SATELLITES," he keyed in.

The screen flashed with a series of coordinates in space. Smith picked the first and locked it into the mode he was using.

"GIVE CODE FOR TRANSMISSION."

"VOICE PRINT REQUIRED," the screen flashed back. "FOR ABRAXAS'S EYES ONLY."

Smith stared at it, feeling numb.

"Do you not like its answer?" Chiun asked solicitously.

"I should have known. The computer's been programmed to screen everyone but Abraxas himself from the data concerning the broadcast."

"Machines are never to be trusted," Chiun said. "We must seek out the false god ourselves."

"There isn't time. He could be broadcasting from anywhere on the grounds." He sat unmoving in front of the computer, his face a blank.

"I will go, emperor."

"Wait," Smith said. "Let me try something." He rearranged the mode on the computer keys.

"GIVE LOCATION OF TRANSMISSION CENTER," he typed.

A blueprint appeared.

"Now it draws pictures," Chiun said irritably.

"This is the layout of the house," Smith said, his eyes scanning the blueprint expertly. When he had memorized it, he turned off the machine and rose. "He's on this floor," he said.

Chapter Sixteen

The trail of Circe's blood led Remo to the rear of the mansion on South Shore. The sea was visible here, roaring behind the deep shadows of the house. Two areas of the place were lit. One wing was bathed in light, and the dim sound of people talking emanated from the brightness. On the opposite end of the manor, a single light glowed from behind a pair of narrow French windows that opened onto the lawn. It was to these windows, directly, that the bloodstains led.

As he neared the source of light, he felt the shadows swallowing him. The place had an aura of perversion and monstrousness about it that made him shiver. It was as if the house itself were alive, infused with the evil of its owner.

Death, Remo was sure, had chosen this place to fold its wings.

The glass doors were open. Inside, Circe lay on a divan, her eyes closed, the front of her dress covered with blood. By her head was a wheelchair facing a paneled wall opposite the windows. Above its leather back Remo could see the top of a man's bald head.

Remo stepped in silently.

"Welcome," a deep voice called from the wheelchair. It was a strange voice, sounding as if it came from an electronic amplifier. A hand motioned toward the wall. "Your shadow gave you away. But then I was hoping you would come."

The wheelchair spun around at a touch from the man's hand to a panel of buttons on the chair's arm. At once Remo recognized the humming, electric sound he had heard in the cave.

The sight was shocking. Circe had told him about her employer's disfigurement, but nothing had prepared Remo for the creature who now stared at him from across the room. He was a man, or had been once. Both of his legs had been amputated at the hip. The trunk above them was strapped into the electric wheelchair by two long leather thongs. His arms were powerfully built. One of them looked normal, the only normal part of his body. The right arm ended in a two-pronged metal claw.

His face was a mass of scars and metal plates grafted over motley skin that had obviously been burned to the bone at one time. He possessed no hair, not even eyebrows. One eye stared roundly out of the lesions; the other was an empty socket discolored to a deep purple-red. His head sat immobile on his neck, which was collared by a thin band of steel. On the band, in the middle of where his throat would have been, protruded a small black box.

"I am Abraxas," he said. The black box vibrated. "I trust you will forgive my appearance. I do not entertain often."

He pressed a button on the wheelchair's arm, and the metal collar moved his head stiffly to the right. "This is Circe, whom you have already met."

Remo walked forward. "It was you," he said.

"At the cave? Indeed it was. Oh, I wouldn't come any closer if I were you." Abraxas jutted his claw hand over the girl's exposed throat. His head was still facing Circe, but his eye was fixed on Remo. "She's alive, you see, and any move you make will change the situation drastically." He laughed, the sound coming low and distorted from the artificial voice box.

Remo halted. "Okay," he said. "What do you want?"

Abraxas's one eye opened wide in mock innocence. "Why, to talk. I wish to talk with both of you. Wake up, Circe. This is for you, too." He jabbed her flesh lightly with the claw. She came awake moaning. "That's better. We can talk now, can't we, my dear?"

She turned toward Remo weakly, her eyes half closed. "Don't stay," she whispered, struggling for breath.

Abraxas shook with laughter. "But of course he'll stay. The man is your lover." He spat out the word with sudden malevolence. "He doesn't want to see you get hurt. Isn't that right ... *Remo*?" The metal claw toyed with her throat.

"She needs a doctor," Remo said.

"You don't know what she needs!" The wheelchair hummed and glided behind the divan in seconds. "I know. I alone. Abraxas." His mouth twisted. "I made you, Circe. And this is how you repay me."

The girl stifled a sob. Her fingers opened and closed on her bloody chest.

"Don't waste your tears. You have no right to them. Have you ever heard of loyalty, Circe?"

"Leave her alone," Remo said.

"Keep out of this," Abraxas hissed. He turned back to Circe, the claw dangling over her face. "I'll tell you about loyalty. When I was a young man, you performed a service for me that enabled me to carry out the work of my destiny—a destiny that was planned for three thousand years, ever since Abraxas, the all-god of the ancients, disappeared into oblivion. He had given up trying to sway men in their corruption, you see. He didn't have the power. But I have." He bent low over her. "I have! Out of the rubble of this body, I created Abraxas anew, Abraxas the perfect god, the giver of life, the force of good and evil, because it was my destiny to do so. For your part in preventing my destruction at the hands of my father, I have given you the world. The *world*!" he shouted.

"I took a servant from the slums of Corinth and gave her a mind. You have traveled the world and lived in splendor. You have received the finest education possible. You have been privy to information that will shape the future of mankind. I have repaid my debt to you, Circe. All I required of you was your loyalty."

He breathed heavily, the claw scraping against her white skin in a sensual rhythm. "Others give their loyalty willingly. At this moment, millions are waiting for just a glimpse of Abraxas. I am their leader. They are depending on me to protect them from their enemies. Enemies like you, Circe. For those who are disloyal to Abraxas are the enemies of all mankind."

"I . . . I should never have saved you," the girl said, weeping. "Your father was right. You should have been destroyed."

"It was not my destiny," Abraxas said softly, craning mechanically toward her face. "It was my fate to live and rule all the people in all the lands of the earth, just as it was my fate to be betrayed by a woman with the lusts of a common slut."

"That's enough," Remo said, stepping forward briskly. Without warning, a thin, bright fiber of electricity shot out from the base of the wheelchair. It struck Remo in the leg, sending him sprawling, dazed, across the room. Circe screamed.

"Do you see how easily life is ended?" Abraxas continued in the same soft voice. "In one moment, the man you thought would save you has ceased to exist. Abraxas gives life, and he takes it away." He raised the claw, crying in despair. "Oh my beautiful, sullied enchantress!"

The claw came down. The body on the divan jerked convulsively, a fountain of blood pouring from her throat.

Remo heard a strangled wail come out from the depths of his soul.

Feeling as if he were dragging himself out of some hideous nightmare, he pulled himself to his feet and staggered toward the other end of the room. Against the wall, he could make out the blurred figure of the creature in the wheelchair.

"You're still alive," the magnified voice said with some surprise.

Remo struggled to focus. Below him lay the woman he had made love to an hour before. Her throat was ripped out brutally. Her eyes stared upward in final terror. The flesh of her face was still warm. *It couldn't be*, he thought, his brain a confused mass of pain and crazy images: Circe huddled in the cave; Circe lying beneath him, her flesh hot and provocative; Circe asking for help, her face lit by the flame of a flickering candle. What was this thing, this slaughtered beast lying dead in front of him? And the man in the wheelchair, a blur, hard to reach . . .

"You'll die for this," he said evenly. "I swear you'll die." Drunkenly, still shaken from the electric shock, he lunged for the wheelchair.

A cloud of white smoke hissed from the chair and filled the room.

A moment later, Abraxas was gone.

Chapter Seventeen

Smith and Chiun both heard Circe's scream. The smoke was clearing from the room as Chiun rushed in through the door to the hallway. Remo was standing near the divan, his eyes fixed on the dead girl drenched in her own blood. His hand was touching her face. He neither moved nor acknowledged the old man.

"What has happened?" Chiun said. "Who has done this thing?"

Remo didn't answer. He lifted his hand from Circe's cheek and closed her eyes.

Smith arrived, panting. "This is it," he said. "This is the room—" He took in the scene. "Oh, no," he said softly, going over to the girl.

Remo stepped away. Then, moving wordlessly along the walls, he smashed every panel systematically, splintering the wood with blows so powerful, they shook the floor.

"Come to your senses," Chiun snapped abruptly.

"I have," Remo said. "The bastard was in a

wheelchair. You would have seen him if he'd left through the door. Remember Big Ed?"

"Big Ed?" Smith asked.

"A hoodlum in Florida," Chiun said. "He used a false floor to escape from us. But this—"

"Circe did say something to me about the house being full of secret passageways," Smith said, looking over at the dead girl. "Did you know her, Remo?"

"Yes."

"I did, too." Smith walked over to her body.

"Forget it," Remo said harshly. He smashed through a panel into dead space. "Here it is. Help me, Chiun." In less than a minute the boards were cleared away.

The opening led into another chamber, also empty, covered with soundproof tiles and hung with a half-dozen black-screened television monitors. A moving camera was stationed in the corner. On the far wall was a digital chronometer that kept time to the second. It was 11:52:45.

"But this room wasn't even on the blueprint," Smith said, bewildered. "I'm sure of it. It pinpointed the location of the transmission area as the room we just came from."

"What are you talking about?" Remo growled as he tapped the walls. "Abraxas said something about showing himself to the world."

Smith explained about the projected midnight broadcast. "He can't be permitted to transmit that message," he warned.

"Look, I want him, too," Remo said levelly.

Suddenly all six of the monitors hanging from

the ceiling flashed into focus. On them were a half-dozen closeups of the disfigured face of Abraxas. He was smiling, his scarred lips twisting grotesquely around his teeth. Smith gave a sharp cry at the sight.

"Admirable, fellows," Abraxas said, the voice box at his throat quivering with sound. "Especially the young one. Why, you should have been killed back there, Remo. Massive electric shocks do that, you know."

"I think you've done enough killing."

"Perhaps." He shrugged. "However, I think that after my broadcast, three new burials will be in order. Four, if you count Circe. Pity."

"You're not going to make any broadcast," Remo said.

Abraxas laughed. "I beg to differ with you. In seven minutes, the god of the new order will come to his people. The name they have been calling in worship will show himself. Not a lovely face for a man, you may say, but sufficiently fearful for the god of good and evil, don't you think?"

"You're a fraud and a murderer," Smith said.

"Ah. The righteous Dr. Smith. You were the thorn in my side I never counted on. Whoever would have taken you for a troublemaker? Well, no matter. My computers were loyal to me even if you weren't."

Smith looked up to the monitor in amazement.

"Oh, yes, I saw you, through a hidden camera, in the computer center trying to unscramble my transmission codes. Very amusing. And the blue-

179

prints, as you see, were false. My whereabouts are out of your reach. In fact, nothing that you, or your genius with computer software, or the remarkable endurance of your young friend Remo can do could ever touch the all-seeing mind of Abraxas."

"You actually believe that garbage of yours, don't you?" Remo said.

"I have every reason to believe it. I am invincible, you see." His face stared at them eerily from the monitors. "I have planned for everything."

"The floor," Remo shouted. He was on his hands and knees, bending over the tiled floor. "There's another passageway here." He ripped off the tiles. Beneath them was a floor of solid cement, etched with a four-by-four-foot square.

"Very good," Abraxas said. "This is indeed the entrance. It is powered by a three-thousand-pound hydraulic lift. The cement itself weighs half a ton."

Remo grunted as he tried to slip his fingers into the hairline crack separating the trapdoor from the rest of the flooring.

"As I was saying, I have planned for everything. Dr. Smith, why don't you try to unscramble my transmission codes? I give you permission."

"You know the access to them is limited to your voice print," Smith said.

"The code is triple zero three one eight zero."

"But why . . ."

"Because I enjoy the edge of challenge. And because, even with help, you still cannot stop me. I told you, I have planned for everything."

A small noise sounded, low and musical at first, then rising higher in pitch and volume until it became a piercing, painful shriek.

"Everything," Abraxas whispered before the word was drowned in the terrible noise.

"What's that?" Smith shouted, covering his ears.

The noise grew worse. Smith fell to his knees, convulsing. In an instant, Chiun was at his side, dragging him through the broken wall. He took Smith into the other room to the door and flung it open.

The noise stopped.

A crowd of people, delegates from the conference, waited outside. At the sight of Smith, they burst into jeers and angry shouts.

"Everything," Abraxas cackled from the monitors.

"Traitor!" the former secretary of state screamed.

"Betrayer!"

"Heretic!"

Through his blurred vision, Smith recognized the advertising man named Vehar. He stepped forward out of the crowd, hefting a rock, and flung it at Smith. The blow took him on the side of his face, scraping off the skin.

"Get me to the computer room," Smith said.

"Yes, emperor." Chiun lit into the crowd like a moving propeller. Vehar spun upward and landed against the corridor wall with a splintering thud. Others threw rocks, but Chiun deflected them with whistling motions of his hands. "Go," he said softly. "I will protect you."

Smith limped away toward the computer room,

like a man twice his age. The wound on his face wasn't deep, but the pain made his head throb.

"Triple zero one three eight zero," he chanted aloud. The eardrum-shattering sound had made him dizzy. Vomit rose in his throat. He forced it down, pushing himself ahead, one foot in front of the other. "Triple zero one three eight zero."

Behind him Chiun was warding off the stampede of delegates, shielding the two of them from their crude weapons. When at last they reached the computer center, Chiun held up a hand to the crowd. "Hold," he ordered. "I am Chiun, Master of the Glorious House of Sinanju, and I warn you—come no farther, or fear for your mortal life."

"He's nothing but a crazy old man," someone shouted from the rear.

"Yeah, and a gook, too."

Vehar pushed his way through the crowd. His jacket was torn. The crystal of his watch was shattered from its impact against the wall. He stepped ahead of the group now, his eyes filled with hate.

"Say, grandpa. I don't think you're so tough."

"Do not use threats lightly," Chiun said. "You should have learned your lesson."

"You got lucky," Vehar said. From his pocket he pulled out a small pistol. The crowd gasped. "And now you're going to get unlucky." He took a quick step forward.

"Forgive me, emperor, but this is necessary," Chiun said. He twisted in the air and, in one deft motion, cracked Vehar's spine and then his skull. The body arched wildly, then fell. Vehar's fingers were still wrapped around the gun.

Smith stood at the console, his eyes riveted on the lifeless body on the floor.

"Work," Chiun commanded the man he called emperor.

"You have four minutes," Abraxas announced, as if Remo were a contestant on a game show who couldn't come up with the right answer.

Remo didn't pay him any attention. He was scrabbling at the cement, his fingertips bloody. Already he had broken off almost enough small pieces to gain a handhold. That was all it would take. But the trap was flush with the floor, and the cement, he guessed, was at least a foot thick.

"Let me save you the effort," the voice said smoothly. "Even if you do get through the trap door—which you won't—you won't be able to reach me. I am an invalid, you see, and don't possess the normal use of my limbs. For this reason, I have had to invent certain architectural designs to assist me. The room you're in is one; I had the trap built. But the room where I am is much more sophisticated. It is closed off from the passageway by a special electronic door housing a million volts of electricity. No one can survive that kind of shock, Remo, not even you. Oh, you surprised me time and again with you strength. The electric jolt from my chair, the high-frequency noise—not a wince from you. Very commendable. But I assure you, the entrance to this room is much more deadly than the parlor tricks I have shown you thus far. Much more. Am I clear?"

"You're an ass," Remo said. With a sharp jab he wedged his left hand into the small crevice he had made. It was tight. The cement rubbed his fingers raw.

"A most worthy opponent," Abraxas said with a certain warmth. "Alas, I have to leave you. I would have liked to see your progress, as well as your untimely end. Unfortunately, my broadcast is due to begin. The world is about to undergo the most profound change since the discovery of fire, and I go to lead its people into the new age. So farewell, my doomed adversary. Enjoy your stay in eternity."

He turned profile to the camera. The face was not so much that of a god as of a gargoyle, Remo thought, a repugnant creature about to spread its slime over the earth.

The monitor faded to black. Remo was alone.

Chapter Eighteen

The chronometer on the wall read 11:58:36. Less than three minutes to go.

He dug his hand deeper into the broken cement. The raw flesh scraped, down to the bone, it seemed. He stifled the urge to cry out with the pain.

11:58:59.

Circe. Abraxas had called her his enchantress. But the girl lying dead in the next room had been nothing but a madman's pawn, discarded without thought, murdered with the casual brutality of swatting a fly.

I don't want to belong to him anymore, she had said. Still, she had kept the name he had given her.

Remo didn't even know her real name.

So this is how it ends, he thought. The twisted trail leading from another death of another pawn named Orville Peabody ended here, with the girl dead and the monster she had hoped to escape safe behind his electric walls.

"You won't belong to him," Remo said. "I promise you, Circe."

He had made a promise to her before, and had not been able to keep it. In shame and rage, he wrenched his arm upward. He felt two bones in his hand crack and give under the weight of the cement, but the slab loosened. With a spray of dust, it spat out of the floor, crashing on the other side of the room.

Beneath the removed cement was a twelve-inch pole extending so far downward that its base couldn't be seen. The hydraulic lift.

11:59:01.

There was no time to find how to operate it. Remo guessed that the controls were on Abraxas's wheelchair, anyway. Keeping his broken hand carefully out of the way, he wrapped his arms and legs around the pole and slid into the darkness.

The bottom was dank and suffocating, exuding the same musty smell of the cave where Remo had lain with Circe. It brought back memories so recent and painful that he felt them physically, like pinpricks in his chest.

But he wouldn't think of her now. He couldn't permit himself the luxury of self-pity.

From the pinpoint opening at the top of the empty shaft, he guessed that he was more than a hundred feet below ground level. He searched in the darkness of the narrow square for a passageway, trying to enlarge his pupils enough to catch what faint light there was.

He saw nothing. No opening, no electric door,

no route to Abraxas. Only the blackness of a four-by-four-foot prison.

Panic crept up on him. What if Abraxas had been lying? True, the cement trap in the floor had been just as he'd described, but a mind as sick as Abraxas's was capable of devising an elaborate obstacle like the trap to serve as nothing more than a diversion for intruders. It was possible that Abraxas was nowhere Remo could reach him before the precious minutes were up. On the other side of the house, perhaps . . . or the island.

I have planned for everything.

More than a minute had passed since Remo began his descent down the lift shaft. Abraxas would have to be reached soon, or not at all. If Abraxas had tricked him, as the sickening feeling in the pit of Remo's stomach told him he had, time had already run out. The world would belong to Abraxas, and Circe—beautiful, scarred enchantress—had died for nothing.

"You idiot," Remo spat out at himself, kicking the cement-lined wall. His foot swung into air.

Air.

He bent down. It was there, the passageway. Abraxas, in his vanity had told the truth. There was a route leading out of the lift, but it was less than three feet tall—designed for a man in a wheelchair.

Flushed with excitement, he ran, stooped, through the dark corridor. There was utterly no light here. Racing blindly, like a bat, he followed the tunnel, ticking off the seconds in his head.

58. 57. 56.

He pumped his legs harder. The pain in his hand throbbed sharply with each footfall. *For Circe*, he said to himself. Not the poor suckers watching their televisions, waiting for God to come to them like some glorious prime-time evangelist; he didn't give a damn about humanity. It was for Circe alone. Dead, defeated Circe, who had begged for help and got none.

His breath came quick and ragged. The passageway was long, longer than he'd pictured the house to be. He'd gone nearly a half-mile as it was, and still nothing lay ahead but more blackness and the growing heaviness in his chest.

What accounted for *that*, he thought, heaving. He never breathed hard. Not even during his exercise runs under Chiun's supervision, in which he forced himself to run at full, leg-wrenching speed over hills so tall that vegetation disappeared at their peaks, had he lost his wind. But now, in this tunnel, he was gasping for breath like a chain smoker in the Boston Marathon.

Still running, crouched and cramping, he attuned his senses to the pressure of the air. He felt it in his ears. Slowly, every fifty feet or so, the pressure increased infinitessimally.

He was running downhill.

And there was a smell permeating the damp cement lining of the tunnel, something pungent, vaguely fishy. . . .

His head shot up with a start. He was heading south, far beyond the reef of the island. What he smelled was the sea. He was underwater.

And going deeper. Abraxas's transmission center was somewhere in the depths of the ocean, protected against unwanted visitors by a million volts of electricity.

26. 25. 24.

Then he saw them, the doors rising out of the blackness like steel monoliths. He could never beat his way through them without electrocuting himself. Even the ways he'd learned for dealing with electric fences wouldn't work with voltage of the magnitude Abraxas had described.

He was unarmed. He looked around helplessly. A piece of cement, maybe, thrown fast enough, could puncture the steel doors, but how much time would that take? He had lost most of the skin on his hand trying to pry loose a small piece of the flooring in the house. It would take even longer to chip a large enough hunk off a smooth wall. Besides, he thought, the hand was broken now. It would be next to useless. No, there was no way through the doors.

Well, *one* way. . . .

He swallowed. Kamikaze had never been his forte. If anything but the soles of his shoes touched those doors, he'd fry in seconds.

He jarred to a halt some twenty feet away from the massive doors. From the size of them, he calculated it would take some six thousand pounds of thrust to break through the electrified metal. Given his weight, that meant that he would have to travel at roughly half the speed of sound to slap on enough pressure to break them down.

Nobody, not Remo, not even Chiun, had ever

moved so fast even at full height. Remo was doubled over in the squat passageway. He would have to run, skittering, like a crab.

Impossible, he decided. It was too big a risk. He'd never live.

He crouched back into the passageway where he'd come, trying to think of alternatives. He forced his mind to a blank. But this time no legends came, no cryptic stories carrying hidden solutions. There was only Circe's face, crying out in the darkness.

Abraxas had won.

"Help me," Circe had said, her remembered voice echoing a memory of a face flickering in candlelight. He had promised to help. Now she was dead, the promise broken.

"Help me . . ."

12. 11. 10 seconds.

"What the hell," Remo said. Maybe he had lived long enough, after all.

He spun around quickly, before he had time to change his mind, and charged the doors.

His arms hung at his sides like an ape's, flying upward behind him as he gathered speed. His feet burned, literally. The heels of his shoes gave off thin wisps of smoke. He felt the flesh of his face flattening, distorting with the speed.

8. 7. 6.

Another image came to mind to replace Circe's face. It was something he'd seen on television once, news footage of an airplane wreck on the Potomac. In the film, a man in a crowd watched from the river's edge as the plane went down. He was an ordinary man, from the looks of him, Mr. Average, football on weekends, maybe a few rounds of cards with the boys on Thursday nights. Nobody would have taken him for a hero.

With the other passersby, he watched the plane crash and burst into flames. Like the others, he heard the screams of the dying. He may have felt pity; the others surely did. Or he may have gone a little crazy at the moment when he took in the sight of the icy river tainted with human blood. No one could say. But what he did at that strange, pivotal moment was so peculiar, so brazen, so unreasonable, that the whole country stopped what it was doing to watch, stunned, as the man did what everyone else had been too sensible to do: *He jumped in.*

He jumped into the freezing, debris-littered water, without any thought for what would happen during the next moment, to rescue a woman who would have died without him.

He lived.

Remo would not live, he was almost sure of that. He was better trained than the man standing on the river's edge, and in a condition superior to any athlete's. But the odds were still a million to one against him that he would approach the *exact* speed at *exactly* the right time, that the impact would be perfect, that the handicaps of a broken hand and excessive air pressure and a snail's posture wouldn't hinder him.

And, somehow, it didn't matter.

Suddenly Remo knew how that man on the river's edge felt, knew as surely as he knew his own name, during that dive into the icy water. There was no heroism involved, no glory, no anticipation, no fear. There was only the air in front of him, and the nerves in his muscles snapping automatically, and the moment he had thrust himself into, pure and free, unconnected with either future or past, moving, soaring, stilled in time.

The doors loomed up ahead of him. Remo grinned. It was going to be one hell of a fine way to go.

Five feet in front of the doors, he propelled himself into a horizontal triple spin. His knees bent instinctively. His hair crackled behind him, lighting the dark tunnel with bright sparks. Then, working purely on reflex, he set himself up for the blow.

The moment had come.

Three. Two. One.

The doors flashed with a boom like a dynamite explosion. Abraxas, seated in his wheelchair facing the camera, looked up in horror.

The room was round and domed. One huge curving window covering half the enclosure looked onto the ocean floor, where primitive dark sting rays fluttered near sponges and red fire coral.

Remo never stopped moving. Rolling into the circular room, he crossed to the curved window in a fraction of a second.

The light on the camera glowed red. Abraxas forced himself to turn toward it. "My—my people," he whispered weakly, his eyes on Remo.

Remo threw himself against the glass, kicking

out with every ounce of strength he could mus-
ter. All he saw now was Circe's face, smiling at
him from the past. So there was a past again, he
thought. And a future. He had lived.

The moment was over.

The glass of the windows starred and burst
outward with the impact from Remo's hurtling
body. The sea, in a fury, rushed into the transmission dome.

He eased his way through the current, his breath
suspended. The water, at this depth nearly as
dark as the tunnel, burst into blinding light as it
reached the electrified doors and set them to
fizzling in a wild fireworks display.

In the sudden brightness he saw Abraxas, first
screaming in terror as the ocean rushed toward
him, then pitching with the force of the water. He
gripped the arms of his wheelchair as it sputtered
and bled white sparks. His one eye rolled back
into its socket, the eyelid quivering spasmodically
as the metal plates on his face and neck blis-
tered and bubbled and steamed in the water.
The last thing Remo saw of him was the black
voice box falling from its brace.

Then the lightning stopped, and a ray floated
lazily into the wreckage.

Chapter Nineteen

Smith was still working frantically at the computer console when Remo arrived back at South Shore. Chiun was standing in the corner, banging at the static-filled television monitor overhead.

"Worthless machine," he grumbled. "No dramas. No news stories. Not even a variety show featuring trained dogs. Only an ugly man being drowned. Probably a commercial."

"What's up?" Remo asked.

"I couldn't scramble the codes in time," Smith said despairingly. "The world got a full ten seconds of Abraxas getting electrocuted underwater. I don't know how the president will ever live this down."

"The president?" Remo said. "What about me? The TV murderer."

"You weren't recognizable," Smith said. "All anyone could see was a blur. How did you get to him, anyway?"

"Well, it was . . ." he began. But the moment had passed. It was over. It would never be the same again, and no one would ever understand what it had been like. "It was a piece of cake," Remo said.

A printout clacked out of the console. "I've sent word to the president about this mess by tapping into the White House computers. This must be his reply," Smith said. He read the printout silently, his face falling. "Helicopters have been dispatched to take out the delegates. Er, I'll have to explain about the casualty. The advertising man."

Smith raised a pencil. "We'll call it an accident. The mental health of the delegates can be proved to be unstable at this point, I think."

"An *accident*? An *ac—*"

"The two of you had better leave the island quickly," Smith said. "No one will believe what they say about Chiun, but I don't want him spotted."

"One does not need to see the Master of Sinanju to recognize his technique."

"Hmmm." Smith looked stricken.

"What's the bad news?"

"Oh, no bad news," Smith said quietly. "The White House press secretary has sent out a bulletin to the news media calling Abraxas's broadcast a hoax. Someone's even confessed to it. Some independent film producer or something."

"Maybe it'll get his name in the papers," Remo said. "But what about the bad vibes Peabody and the other zombies caused? You said the United Nations was up in arms."

Smith took a deep breath. "It seems that problem is solved, too. New terrorists have come in to replace the assassinated leaders. The countries who were accusing other world powers of sabotaging their images are back to working on the terrorist problem again."

"Back to normal, huh?"

"Normal," Smith muttered, more to himself than anyone else.

"Of course it is normal," Chiun said. "Chaos must be maintained to balance order. It is the inviolate principle of Zen. Good and evil, yin and yang. It has existed long before the fraud who called himself Abraxas."

"What about Circe?" Remo asked suddenly.

"I'll arrange to have her buried. We won't be able to attend the funeral, of course."

"Then who will?" Remo asked. "No one even knew her name."

The room fell silent. At last Smith spoke. "It will be a civil burial, I imagine."

"You mean a pauper's burial. Something for the bums nobody cares about."

In the distance, carried over the sea, could be heard the faint drone of helicopters.

"A special plane is coming to take me to Washington," Smith said crisply, dropping the subject of funerals. His silence spoke louder than words. *After all, there's nothing anyone can do about her now.* "I suggest that the two of you head back toward Folcroft as soon as possible. Can the boat you took me on get you as far as Miami?"

"It'll get us as far as Trinidad," Remo said.

"Also Haiti, Puerto Rico, Guadelupe, Barbados, Jamaica . . ."

"Out of the question," Smith snapped.

"I have a broken hand."

"We'll see to it at Folcroft." He rose to turn off the computer console.

"I also have your plans to rip off the IRS," he said.

Smith looked over to him, gaping. "What are you saying?"

"You heard me. It was happy hour with the dictator of the world, remember? Either Chiun and I cruise the seas until my hand gets better, or the Internal Revenue boys get a little present from Harold W. Smith."

"That's blackmail!" Smith sputtered.

"Hey, nobody hired me for this job because I was a nice guy."

"You're walking a thin edge, Remo."

"Tell it to the judge," Remo said.

Once outside the computer room, he touched Chiun's arm. "You go back to the ship, Little Father," he said. "I've got something to do."

The old man's face creased. "Do not punish yourself, my son. Some things cannot be helped."

"I know," Remo said.

He walked back to the room where Circe lay. Her body had stiffened in death. The long scar on her face stood out darkly against her white skin.

"Enchantress," he said, lifting her gently.

He carried her through the French windows to the grounds outside, breaking easily through the wire fence surrounding South Shore. The clouds had passed, and the night sky was again illuminated by the sparkle of a million tiny stars.

He took her back to the cave where they had loved together. Inside, he dug a grave deep in the cave's recesses, where the scents of moss and the sea belonged.

"Good-bye, Circe," he said, and kissed her on her cold lips. For a moment they seemed to come alive again, warm and loving. But the sensation vanished, and he laid her body to rest.

He covered the burial mound with colored stones and a starfish he found at the ocean's edge. Then he stood back, proud of his work. The grave was a small enough monument to the girl with no name, but it was for him, too. For one day, he knew, he would also be an unknown body with no identity. Like Circe, he possessed none in life. His death, surely, would be just as anonymous as hers.

And so he buried her for both of them.

He walked out of the cave slowly. At the entrance, he thought he heard something and turned back, but the place was silent. Fitting for a tomb.

It was not until he was well away, walking through the mild surf of the darkened beach, that it came to him again, soft but unmistakable, the work of the wind and the sea in the echoes of a rocky inlet marked by a starfish: music.

The cave was singing, and its music was a siren's song.

CELEBRATING 10 YEARS IN PRINT
AND OVER 22 MILLION COPIES SOLD!